THE VISITOR AT WINTER CHAPEL

THE
VISITOR
AT WINTER
CHAPEL

~ *A NOVEL* ~

MICHELLE BATCHELER
AND FRANK SIKORA

MBF Press
Montgomery

MBF Press
105 South Court Street
Montgomery, AL 36104

Library of Congress Cataloging-in-Publication Data
ISBN-13: 978-0-9785311-7-1
ISBN-10: 0-9785311-7-5

Printed in the United States of America

To Mom and Dad

FOR THEIR LOVE, SUPPORT, AND MOTIVATION TO DREAM BIG

— M.B.

To My Family, Here and Beyond

— F. S.

Prologue, January 2006

After a day of rain and a raw, whistling wind that chilled the bones, the skies had cleared. Colder air was now sweeping in, whipping the few russet leaves that clung precariously to the bare branches of the old sweet gum tree. It was typical winter weather for Alabama.

From the living room window I watched with awe as the afternoon sun suddenly put a reddish glow on the tree trunks out front. It was the picture of peace.

And then a white van eased into the driveway. It had electronic gear jutting out from the top. The letters "CNN" were inscribed on the side.

I shook my head and forced a weary smile. "Here we go again."

My mother heard me and hurried in from the kitchen. "More news people, Abbie?" she asked.

"Oh, yeah," I said. "Don't worry, Mom, I'll go out and talk with them. I'll only be a minute. After all, a college sophomore should be able to deal with the news media."

"Are you going out like that?" she asked. "Sweatshirt and jeans?" Before I could say anything about my casual attire, she added, "I just don't understand why they keep coming around."

"Be of good cheer, Mom. That's what I want to do someday." Then I went out on the porch.

A young woman wearing a khaki all-weather coat alighted

from the van. She was followed by a man in a gray suit. Behind them came a slim, balding fellow wearing jeans and an Army field jacket. He held a camera. I went out to meet them.

"Are you Miss Staley?" the woman called. "Abbie Staley?"

I folded my arms tightly against the cold. "Yes, that's me. Can I help you?"

"Well, we hope," she said, as they drew nearer. "We've been told that some kind of—of unusual event—"

"Like a miracle?" I suggested ruefully.

"Right, like a miracle," she said, her face brightening. "Some kind of miracle happened here and we were wondering if you would talk with us. I mean talk on camera."

With that, the guy in blue jeans began to film me. It was a bit sudden, but I raised no objection.

"Well, I'm not sure who saw what," I said, giving the cameraman a cold glance. "But it seems to me that miracles happen all the time, and people either don't recognize them, or—"

"The Birmingham paper said that people were here in the field singing carols and holding candles," the woman said. "Was that on the night of December twenty-third?"

I shrugged and focused on her. "I think that was the night. Of course, people sing carols around here at Christmas time."

"Two thousand of them?" she quizzed, her eyebrows raised. "We heard there were two thousand people here."

"That figure came from the state troopers," I replied. "I didn't count."

Then the man in the suit stepped forward. "The Birmingham paper also quoted a man to say he saw you talking . . . well, talking with someone who looked like . . . like Jesus Christ." He gave an impatient shrug and a quizzical grin. "Is that true? Was he here? Did you talk to him in Birmingham, too? Or was it just on that hill back there?"

I smiled and shook my head. "Of course, I talk to Jesus every day. A lot of people do. What people say they saw is for them to explain."

"So you won't confirm or deny the reports," the man pressed.

"Hey, 'confirm or deny?' Come on." I laughed outright. "This sounds like a presidential press conference."

"Well, do you?"

"Yes . . . yes, I can't confirm or deny, because, as I said, I believe miracles occur all the time, and I do talk with Jesus every day."

The woman folded her arms and took a step closer. "Did you actually talk to him . . . or are you telling us that you 'talk' when you pray?"

"Yes, that's correct."

She flashed a puzzled smile. "*What's* correct?"

"What you were just saying," I said, still smiling.

"Why are you smiling at everything we ask?" she said.

"I guess I'm just happy," I declared. "But y'all are welcome to photograph the hill back of the house if you want. That's where the cherry trees are."

She stared at me with a chilly smile. Then, throwing an exasperated wave at me, she led them around to the back. I retreated to the house.

My mother waited at the door. "Are they leaving? Oh, I hope we don't get a mob here looking for a miracle."

"I think they're filming out back," I said. "They wanted to see the hill."

The hill.

I

For as far back as I can remember, the grassy hill was a place of wonder, a retreat where a child could dream or just run up and down and laugh. It was my favorite place in the world. It rose above our farm house and overlooked the garden my dad always planted.

There were three cherry trees on the far right side of the hill. In the springtime they always had the most lavish display of pinkish-white blossoms. My mother had planted a row of daffodils around the front of them. It was quite a dazzling sight. When I was five or so, she told me the blossoms were put on the trees by angels. I believed it then . . . and I still do.

My name is Abigail Staley, although everyone calls me Abbie.

Many afternoons my brother, Austin, and I would sit on the hillside watching clouds roll by in shapes that looked like dragons and bears. But after an hour or so we would start wondering what our mother was cooking for supper. And we would race down the hill. Austin, who was two years older, always let me win.

Big brothers always let kid sisters win.

Our home was just outside the hamlet of Winter Chapel, Alabama.

The house had belonged to my grandfather. When he died, my parents took over the farm. Grandmother had died earlier, when I was much younger. My dad was not a full-time farmer. He and my mother just liked rural life and so did Austin and I.

Actually, Dad worked for an insurance company and had an office in the house. The farm had about fifty acres to it; we rented out about half to a man who raised soybeans.

The house was built in the 1930s. It was a two-story frame structure with a wrap-around front porch which was furnished with a swing and two rocking chairs. Out back, beside the garden, was a sagging red barn where Dad kept an old John Deere tractor that no longer ran.

My room, located in the back part of the upstairs, had a shelf full of dolls. The white dresser held two things: a pink angel on one side, and a picture of Jesus on the other. The angel, I was told, had been in the family for ages.

Our home was a cozy, safe haven as Austin and I were growing up. We felt somebody would always be watching over us. Our parents would be there . . . the house would be there . . . the hill would always be there . . . and Jesus would be above somewhere, looking down on us.

By the time we were in high school, Austin was almost a dead ringer for a young Tom Hanks, at least in my book he was. He had dark curly hair and blue eyes. He was about six-two. I had grown to be about five-eight; my hair was a honey-blonde shade, which I wore about waist length. I took after my mother, whose hair was light. My brother's darker strands were more like our father's.

When I was starting my sophomore year, Austin was a senior. I was fifteen then, he was seventeen. It was 2001. For me it meant spending more time dwelling on my future. I had already made up my mind to go to college and study journalism. My dream was to be a television anchor. I wanted to be like the young women on the Birmingham stations, or those on the Weather Channel. But I wanted to develop ultimately into another Barbara Walters.

Then came September 11, the day the world changed for everyone. Dad came to the school and signed both of us out for the day. He said Mom was afraid terrorists might strike schools or other public sites.

Like everyone in the nation we were glued to the television looking at the scenes from New York and Washington. I was horrified by the sight. But it was far away, I reasoned.

"Mom," I said. "They wouldn't come all the way down to Alabama to attack a little school, would they?"

"You never know," she replied tightly, her eyes on the screen.

"Well, that does it," snapped Austin. "I've made up my mind. I'm joining the Army when I graduate."

"No you are not, young man!" Mom shot back with more anger than I had ever seen in her. It made her eyes blaze. "You're going to college."

"I don't want to go to college," he said, the voice still edged with subdued fury. "I want to be a soldier, Mom. We're in a war, whether we like it or not."

But she was not giving an inch. "You can't go in unless we sign for you. Isn't that right, Jeff?"

My father was a man of medium build, and at age forty-five was starting to put a bit too much weight around the middle. He blocked any further debate.

"Son, your mother is right," he said calmly. "Let's wait until you're eighteen to decide about the Army, okay?"

"Dad, you see that?" Austin gestured toward the television, as it repeated the scene of a plane crashing into one of the twin towers.

"I know, I know," my father said. "But even if you go today, it would be six months or so before you'd be trained. And who do we fight? The terrorists on those planes are already dead, son.

Another few months of waiting won't hurt you. The Army's not going away. There will be plenty of time to get in on things, if being a soldier is what you want."

Austin glanced at me, then back at our father. "That's what I want."

I stared at my brother a long time. He never became angry. He loved country music and also liked some light classics as well as movie soundtracks. He often studied as he listened to the score from *The Last of the Mohicans,* which was something he did not mention to friends. And while he liked both Auburn and Alabama, his favorite college football team of all-time was Princeton's 1950 and '51 squads. He had pictures of Dick Kazmaier and Frank McPhee on his wall. They were his heroes.

But now we were talking about him joining the military. This scene didn't seem real. We shouldn't be talking about him joining anything—not the Army, not the Marines, not anything. But it was happening. Austin was just not cut out to be a soldier, I thought.

As we watched the horror from New York and Washington, Mom abruptly rose and shut the television off. "I don't want to look at that anymore." And with that, she went into the kitchen.

2

That Sunday we went to church, joining the others in our community to pray about what was happening in our country, and to pray for those who died in the terrorists' attack. I was glad Mom and Austin had called a cease-fire over his future in the military.

Winter Chapel is a crossroads community of about four hundred souls. The economic anchor is Pop Jackson's General Store, a sprawling white frame building which also houses the U.S. Post Office. On any given day you could go to the store and catch up on what was going on around the world, the state, or just here in Winter Chapel. Usually Pop was the moderator, but a farmer named Aaron Jefferson was always on hand to give his views—loudly and endlessly.

Across the road is Fleming's gas station. The county school lies about a mile south of the intersection. Within a quarter-mile are three churches, the cemetery, the volunteer fire department, a small health clinic, and Janet's beauty salon.

It is beautiful country, with small hillside farms dotting the landscape. The roads are fringed with a variety of trees. In the autumn flaming sumac bushes lead the colorful changes that run from late September through early December. In the early spring the redbud trees splash purple-red sprays that contrast with the gaunt hardwoods and the evergreens.

The area had been settled in the 1840s by a Methodist minister, James Winter, and his family. One of the first things he did was build a small chapel. It still stands today, although it has undergone many renovations over the years.

While there are three churches, there are not enough members in each to pay a full-time minister, so each denomination has one come out every three weeks. We rotate the services from church to church. One Sunday we all go to the Baptist Church to which we belong. The next we would go to the Methodist and the third it would be the Presbyterian.

This is sometimes confusing for me, but when it comes right down to it we all believe in Jesus Christ. That Sunday I paid little heed to the sermon, but instead closed my eyes and asked Jesus to watch over us as always, and especially my brother. Things were happening too fast for me. It seemed certain that we were going to be in a war. Where, I didn't know, but it was surely coming.

Of course, it was clear that everything was changing anyway . . . we were getting older, and the carefree days of climbing the little grassy hill and day-dreaming about life were coming to an end. Austin would meet a girl he liked, get married, and one day I would be an aunt.

As for myself, I didn't think too much about meeting anyone, or marriage, anything like that. I wanted a career in television. These thoughts went through my head.

After church that day, we had dinner. It was Mom's fried chicken and mashed potatoes, and a sweet potato pie. We had a lot to be thankful for.

The days flew by then. There were the Friday night football games which we always attended. Austin was a wide receiver. He was good, making great catches, and being a solid team player. But his mind was no longer on football and trying for a spot on a college team. He had talked about being a history teacher one day, but even that was now something he put on hold. We had already sent troops to Afghanistan. Austin's mind was focused on being a soldier.

So on a balmy May evening in 2002 we went to his graduation. It was one of those days when an afternoon rainfall cleared the air and left the world flooded in the fragrance of lilacs and honeysuckle. It was during the ceremony that it dawned on me that April had passed and I had scarcely noticed the cherry blossoms on the hill.

A few days later, Austin, who had turned eighteen in March, went to the Army recruiting station and signed up.

On the evening before he was to leave, we walked up to the hillside as we had done as children.

"Well, brother, are you getting a little nostalgic yet?" I was trying to sound grown-up. But a sixteen-year-old is still a kid sister, and would always be one.

"I guess a little." Then he turned serious. "You know I'll miss you, Abbie, and Mom and Dad. And this place."

"Times two." I said. It was a phrase we always used. It meant "same here" or "right back at you."

"Yeah, times two," he said reflectively. Then, "You help Mom now, you hear?"

"I will, I promise." I pulled a weed and chewed on it a moment. "You know where you'll go?"

"Fort Benning at first." He shrugged. "After that, I don't know."

I avoided talking about his chances of going to Afghanistan, where our troops were searching for terrorists.

For a long time we sat on the hill, just staring down at the house.

Then, after a long pause, he said something that I found surprising, for Austin wasn't a melodramatic guy. "You know, this place up here is . . . is sort of sacred ground for us."

"For us it is, I guess," I agreed. "It sure is. It's a peaceful place."

He didn't look at me. "Remember when we were kids, coming up here?"

"Yeah. I'll never forget those days. Or these."

We sat in silence. Then Mom called, "You guys come down for supper."

Austin grinned. "Now that I will miss."

As we stood, I looked down at the ground. "I'll write to you; let you know what's going on." Then I blurted it out, "And I will pray for you. We've never been away from home before, neither of us. I'll miss you."

He nodded. "Times two."

Then he put an arm around my shoulders for a moment. Suddenly he let go and shouted, "Race you down!"

I squealed and ran as fast as I could. As always, he let me win.

3

So Austin went into the Army, and trained and trained. Sometimes he would call, and sometimes he would write letters. I started my junior year in the fall of 2002. Every Sunday we would go to church and pray for peace, and for Jesus to watch over my brother.

We were worried that he might have to go to Afghanistan, although the U.S. force there was rather small. Then, in March 2003, American forces invaded Iraq, based on reports that the Iraqis had weapons of mass destruction, and that the Iraqi leaders were connected to the 9-11 attacks. Our concern for Austin increased. This was a much larger military operation.

I didn't know much about history and war, but it seemed to me that this was the first time America was fighting on two fronts since World War Two—Afghanistan and Iraq. At the beginning in Iraq we were fighting Saddam Hussein's army, and then later battling the so-called insurgents. The situation left me confused. It wasn't working out the way the political leaders said it would.

By May 2004 I was a senior, ready to graduate and take my place in the big world.

More than a year had passed since American troops had been in Iraq, but we had been lucky. Austin had not been sent to either Iraq or Afghanistan. He had been in the Army for two years. We were afraid his time would come to go to Iraq, where

American soldiers were being killed at the rate of two or three a day, mostly by roadside bombs.

Our fears proved to be right. Austin, who had been helping in training soldiers at Fort Ord, California, sent us a letter not long after I graduated. It was what we dreaded. He was on orders for Iraq.

"My number just came up," he wrote. "Everyone's does sooner or later."

He had been home on leave a few months earlier. On that visit we walked up the hill and he had told me he was getting tired of training recruits.

"That's not why I joined," he told me.

"That's not your call," I reasoned. "You follow the Army's orders. They tell you to train recruits, you train recruits. Right?"

"You'd make a good sergeant," he said, chuckling.

"Times two," I replied.

So I was certain he had volunteered, but decided not to tell Mom and Dad. My brother had his own path to follow. It mattered little whether he volunteered or not. The fact was he was going to a war zone. In July 2004 he was on a plane for Iraq.

That summer I worked part-time helping children in a reading class held at the school. It brought in a little money for college. In August I began classes at the University of Alabama at Birmingham, UAB for short. My parents drove me there and I got a room in a dormitory, meeting my roommate.

Her name was Ginger Burns. She was a slim, dark-haired girl from a rural community in the southern half of the state. She was going to major in business management, although she wasn't quite sure. I felt I was one up on her because I was certain of my major and the eventual direction of my life.

We were to become best friends. Ginger had a way with words. In fact, she talked up a storm the day we met, as though she had known us for all of our lives. Mom and Dad liked her and invited her to come home with me some weekend.

"Oh, I'd like that," Ginger gushed. "I'm partial to small towns. And the moms usually can cook with the best of them."

"We don't exactly live in a town," I explained. "It's just a place. You know, rural crossroads and all." But it would be nice, I thought, having a roommate coming home with me.

Along with my studies I became connected with a campus Christian group. We met every Tuesday night and sometimes we joined protests at abortion clinics. It was something I was starting to get passionate about. I did not agree with Supreme Court rulings which allowed abortions on demand. The protests were not noisy or violent; we simply prayed.

One of the leaders was a junior named Glenn Lyons, a quiet-spoken guy who resembled a younger Clark Kent, even to the point of fidgeting with his glasses when he was nervous or uncertain. Nervous and uncertain was a common trait when the police threatened to arrest us at one protest. That's when Glenn told us all to move back and walk away.

After one such protest I wrote Austin a letter telling him how involved I had become with the issue. "You are over there fighting for freedom for the Iraqi people, while we allow killing of babies over here. If I had my way, we would bring the troops home to protect the unborn babies."

He wrote back:

Dear Sis:

I read your letter about the abortion protests. I don't know what to think about anything anymore. Over here it is heat and dust and killing, and I have seen more than I want to. We go on patrols and people in civilian clothes shoot at us, or they set off bombs when we go by. Don't tell Mom, but one went off the other day and a piece of it nicked my arm. A guy near me, a friend, was badly hurt and may not live. He is only 19. I'm okay, but it was close. I feel Jesus will watch over me here. But I will be glad to be back home one day. Abbie, I have to shoot and I pray that I never hit a child. That scares me to death. I saw a place that our planes struck the other day and there were little children in there. It was awful. Stay on the abortion issue if the spirit says to. Have there been any protests against this war? I miss you. I hope you study hard and always follow your heart and mind. Wish we could just sit on the hill and watch the clouds.

Love, Austin

4

ecember 2004. Ginger was as happy and carefree as ever. Our friendship grew stronger, but there was an invisible shield around her that kept me from getting too close on issues that were important to me. I tried to get her into the Tuesday night Christian group, but she said she preferred not to be involved, because it meant protesting abortion.

"I don't want to take a chance on getting arrested or something," she said.

"Well, you don't have to go to the protests with us," I explained. "I think you just might enjoy talking with some of the people. There are other things besides abortion protests."

"I believe in women having a choice," she declared gently, but with a firm resolve.

"Well, I agree, roomie," I parried. "The choice should be not to do something that gets her pregnant."

"You're just an old-fashioned girl, aren't you, Abbie," she chided.

"I guess that's true." I was a little defensive. "That's how I was raised."

And it was. We let the issue drop then, but not before the point was made that my interests included more worldly things.

For instance, there was the need of a nice car. I had talked to my dad about it. Being away from home was new for me. I might want to drive home some weekends. It was only about seventy-five miles east of Birmingham.

"Well, we can take a look," Dad had promised.

So one evening in December he drove to Birmingham and took me to supper. Afterwards we went to a used-car lot. He picked out a 1991 Cutlass with a new coat of green paint.

I didn't want to appear ungrateful, but I wasn't exactly thrilled. It was the kind of vehicle that got heads turning . . . because of the distinct clatter it raised. Threshing machines made less of a ruckus.

But Dad insisted, "It'll be a dependable car for you."

I nodded.

"Shoot, I wouldn't be afraid to start off for California in that thing," he said.

"Dad I am not going to California. I just want to get to Winter Chapel once in a while."

But he stuck to his choice; I got the Cutlass and drove it back to the campus, while Dad headed home. In a somewhat depressed mood, I entered the dorm room and tossed my jacket on the bed and flopped down.

"Well, I got a car," I told my roommate. "It's a real clunker. I'll take you for a ride in it tomorrow . . . just in case it needs a push."

The phone rang, interrupting my sour mood. It was Mom, and she was talking so fast and loud I could not understand her.

"Mom, slow down," I said. "Run that by me again."

"Austin called from Iraq," she cried. "He says he may get to come home for Christmas, but he's not sure. He is okay. He couldn't talk long."

"He may get to come home?" I was elated. "That's great! Things are looking up, Mom."

After hanging up, I turned to Ginger. "You hear that? My brother might get to come home for Christmas."

I waited for a snappy response. But all I heard was a subdued, "That's nice."

She was sitting on the side of her bed and glumly brushing her hair. I propped up on my elbow and stared at her.

"Something the matter?" I asked.

"No," she said. "Why would you ask me that?"

I shook my head. "No reason, except you usually have something to say. You just don't seem your bright, adorable self tonight."

She ignored my attempt at humor. In fact, she pulled the covers loose and got into her bed, turning away from me. It was so unlike her.

"Little early to turn in, isn't it?" I pressed.

She didn't answer. Something was wrong, and I was snoopy enough to find out what it was.

"Hey, roomie," I said. "How about going home with me this weekend. You'll like the place, and my mom is the best cook in Winter Chapel. You'll enjoy the ride."

No reply. Then, "You go. I . . . I get car sick real easy. And I don't want to hear any lectures."

"Lectures?" I sat up and gazed at the back of her head. "What are you talking about? I haven't lectured you about anything."

Now she turned over and looked at me. I noticed her eyes were red. She had been crying.

"Ginger, what's wrong?" I asked. "I know something's wrong."

She let out a deep breath and stared at the floor. Then, "Were you born yesterday? Can't you tell . . . I'm pregnant. I went to see some people today about it."

It floored me. "Pregnant! Are you sure? Good gosh, who

. . . you hardly dated anyone that I know of." I was flustered by the news. It was extra upsetting because she was hinting at an abortion.

"It's somebody I met at a class," she said. "I had a drink or two. Is that a sin?"

"Well, I don't know," I said, still reeling from the news. "It just depends."

"Yeah, yeah, it depends," she said sarcastically. "Well, I'll tell you the only thing that depends on anything is that I'm in trouble. I can't let my parents know about this. I can't."

"You're not in trouble," I said. "My brother is in Iraq. Now that's real trouble. You have options. You can put the baby up for adoption. There are people out there who are trying to adopt a child and raise it. Good people. Don't be a part of killing a baby."

Now Ginger was on her feet. Her demeanor had changed and she was almost combative.

"Oh, yeah, there's innocent Abbie with all the answers," she snapped. "Just read the Bible and listen to the preachers rant about things, and you got all the answers. It's so simple for you."

"Hey, there's no reason to get mad at me," I shot back. "You got yourself into this."

I got up from the bed and grabbed my jacket. There was nothing to be gained by arguing with her. And I couldn't horn in on her personal life by calling her parents.

So I left and went for a drive. I had worked up some steam, but there was no use making things worse for her. After all, she was my friend.

Maybe I could get some of the people in the group to talk to her. But she was in a mess, one had to admit.

I was too young to be worrying about things like this. But here it was, right in front of me. I stopped by a convenience store and had an icy drink, then, after about a half-hour, went back to the dorm.

Ginger was sitting on her bed, head down, reading a letter. She glanced up at me. "Sorry, I blew up at you," she said.

"That's okay," I said, trying to take the edge off my voice. "No harm done."

"We still friends?" she asked.

I looked at her and nodded. "Sure we are."

She smiled. "I'm glad, Abbie, and sorry I yelled at you. You're my very best friend."

It melted me. "Times two."

"Times two for me, too." She tossed the letter aside. "It's just that I don't know what to do."

"I know how you feel." Then I shrugged. "Well, I don't know how you feel exactly."

It drew a faint smile from her. "What do you think I should do?"

I shook my head. "Ginger, do you think the first thing is to let the expectant father know about this?"

She pondered it, but said nothing. She was waiting on more from me, but I didn't want to be preaching. "What about your parents, you think you should tell them soon?"

She winced. "I think it would kill them."

She was a young woman, but in some ways a child. I sat beside her and put an arm around her shoulder. I had one answer to her dilemma. She probably didn't want to hear it.

"Maybe you should try prayer," I said. "Sometimes it helps."

She shrugged. "You think that might do some good? I've never been much for that stuff."

"Look, why don't you call your folks and tell them you're coming home with me for Christmas," I said. "It's just a couple of weeks off. You could talk with my mom."

"No, I couldn't do that," she said haltingly. "Swear you won't say anything to her, please. Promise? "

"Well, okay, if that's what you want," I said. "Promise. But you really can't tell anything by looking at you. I mean, you're still trim and slim."

"I think mothers can always tell," she said, twisting her fingers as she wrestled with the problem. "Maybe I'll just tell my folks that I'm going home with you for Christmas. But I will stay here."

5

I remained with Ginger through most of the lonely days of the holiday break. The place was deserted, almost ghostlike. I hated to leave her alone, but on the morning of Christmas Eve, I headed for home. I made one last futile appeal for her to come with me.

As I drove through the morning sunshine, I thought about the family gathering. We still had not heard anything certain from Austin. But there was time.

Part of my attention, however, was on the Cutlass . . . it sounded like I was driving a car with a bunch of rusty saw blades scraping against one another. Still, it moved along. I decided it would be a good time to talk to Mom about Ginger's situation. After all, it wasn't breaking a promise for a girl to talk to her mother. Right?

Arriving in Winter Chapel was like stepping into a Hallmark card. There were Christmas decorations and manger scenes everywhere. A small pond in a meadow looked like a mirror reflecting the azure sky. What a good feeling it brought. I hummed some carols. I loved Christmas carols. It was a beautiful change of pace from what I usually listened to.

As I pulled into the driveway I was amazed at the effort Mom had put into decorating our old country home. She made it look like it should be in a magazine. She was going all-out because Austin might be coming home. But wow! I had never seen it look so pretty, so inviting and warm. What a great holiday it was going to be!

The pebbles on the driveway crunched under my tires, and tossed up against the underside of the car. I noted that the marigolds alongside the house had finally turned brown. I was hoping to see a rental car in back, a sign that Austin had made it home. But, there was nothing but Mom's blue Ford. Dad's pickup was gone.

Getting out of the car, I glanced up at the hill. The tall grass was a faded golden-brown, tossing slightly in the light breeze; the cherry trees were dark, twisted things. But there was a warmth to it and it made me smile. Even in the dead of winter, it was a special place. It would be good to be with Austin going up and just talking like old times.

I pulled my things out of the car. On the back porch, I caught the aroma of baked goods from the kitchen. It was my first time ever to be coming home for Christmas. In the past, I had always just been here.

As I walked in, Mom rushed to give me a hug before a word could be spoken about anything. Then as quickly, she turned and scurried back to the stove. For certain, Mom had caught the spirit of the season.

"Merry Christmas, Mom," I cried belatedly, putting my suitcase down. "You been in the kitchen all day?"

"I started last night," she called, laughing. "You should have been here."

Pausing, I twisted the graduation ring on my finger. Actually, I should have been here, I thought, but it was also important that someone be with Ginger. She faced a lonely holiday.

"Have we heard from Austin yet?"

"No, not yet," she said, gazing into the oven, "But your daddy thinks he is going to surprise us. Oh, I hope he's right."

I went to my room to put my things away, and then hurried back to the kitchen.

"Can I help?" I couldn't remember ever being allowed to do much with the cooking, although she did allow me to wash dishes.

"You can set the table," she replied.

"You don't trust me with helping with the food?" I joked. "Your favorite daughter?"

"Go on," she said waving a dish towel at me.

As I got some dishes from the cabinet, I asked, "So Dad thinks Austin will just pop in, huh?"

That would be like Austin, I thought. Just show up at the door in time to eat. That would be just fine with me.

"Well, how's school going?" she asked. It was clear she was avoiding any thought that Austin might not make it.

"I guess okay; it's pretty stressful, though," I said. "It seems I spend as much time worrying about my friends as I do about my studies."

Mom shot a puzzled look at me "What do you mean?"

"Well, really it's just Ginger," I said. "She really concerns me."

Mom tossed the dish towel over her shoulder and sat down at the kitchen table. It was the signal for me to start talking.

"Okay. Ginger is . . . well, okay, she asked me not to say anything," I confided, stumbling over the words. "But she is pregnant. There, I said it. That's the problem that concerns me. She's scared to tell her parents, and who can blame her?"

Mom blinked a couple of times in surprise. "Ginger's going to have a baby? How—I mean, when did this happen?"

"I don't know, Mom. She's . . . well, what concerns me is she's talking about having an abortion."

"Oh, no, no," Mom cried, shaking her head. "Why would

she want to do that? You talk to her."

"I tried to explain to her that there are other things she can do," I said. "But she's just so dang headstrong. You can't tell her anything, you know?"

Mom surprised me with her response. "Abbie, maybe you shouldn't try to tell her what to do. Don't be too preachy. Just be her friend, not her coach. That's what she really needs right now, a friend. I think Ginger has a good head on her shoulders."

"I agree, but, wow, Mom, this is a major-league problem, you know?"

"Welcome to the real world, young lady," she said with a sad smile. "It doesn't get any easier."

"I know it is the real world, but someone needs to help," I said. "You just can't leave her alone out there."

At that moment, we heard a car door slam. A few seconds later someone was stomping on the back porch. I jumped up, thinking it might be Austin. But Dad came in, and we knew it was time to stop talking about Ginger's problems.

Mom vaulted up from the table and scooted to the stove to check on the food.

"Smells like some good cookin' goin' on in here." Dad called loudly, rubbing his stomach. "I see our college girl made it home."

"Yeah, Dad, barely," I said. "We need to do something with that car."

"Nothing wrong with that car," he said, laughing, and giving me a hug. "We hear anything from Austin, yet?"

"Not yet, but you know Austin," I said.

Then I returned to the task of setting the table.

In our home, we always had a big Christmas Eve supper. That was one of the few times we used the dining room. Usually we just ate in the kitchen. But Christmas Eve was special . . .

and this one would be even more so. The feast would be roast beef, whole potatoes and carrots cooked in the beef juice, celery, and homemade bread, plus apple and cherry pie. That was the traditional fare for the gathering.

After finishing the table-setting, and while Mom and Dad were talking in the kitchen, I eased out the side door. There wasn't a lot of money for gifts, but I had picked up a few things which were hidden in the trunk. It was a good time to sneak them into the house and place them under the tree.

I undid the trunk and was gathering them up when a car turned into the driveway. I rose up and turned.

It was an Army car. Austin!

6

I screamed, "Mom! Dad! Austin's here!" My shrill call brought Mom rushing out the screen door. She was in such a hurry that the door slammed behind her hitting Dad so quickly that his glasses were almost knocked off. For a moment I almost laughed. Then I turned around again.

The doors of the Army car opened and two soldiers got out.

I stared in surprise. "Where's Austin?"

They exchanged puzzled glances. "Ma'am?" one of them said.

I stood gaping at them. "I thought it was my brother. Is he here?"

And then it dawned on me that they were here about Austin, but not with him. Why were they here?

"They don't come to your house unless something bad has happened," Dad called out from behind me.

"What's going on?" I asked, my eyes still on the soldiers.

"Mr. and Mrs. Staley?" one of them said, addressing Mom and Dad. I later learned he was a captain. "Are you Mr. and Mrs. Staley?"

My mother's jubilant mood faded quickly into a pale, distressed look. Then suddenly she became hysterical. "Oh, no. Oh, no."

Dad grabbed her shoulders to keep her steady.

I clung to some hope that it was about Austin being slightly wounded. "Maybe it's not real bad, Mom," I called.

Then we went into the house and I kept asking, "What's going on? Is something the matter?"

The soldiers entered the living room behind us, removing their caps.

I watched as Mom dropped to her knees and bowed over, almost touching the floor with her face. She was now wailing, "It's Austin. It's Austin."

"Mom, Mom," I cried. "Maybe he's been wounded or something."

But then I heard the captain telling Dad, "Sir, we need to talk to you and your wife. Why don't you have a seat there on the couch."

"Oh, no," Mom wailed. "Not my boy."

The two of them leaned over and helped Mom to stand. She grabbed onto Dad's arm, burying her face into his chest.

"Won't you sit down, please," the captain urged.

"Just tell us!" Dad cried out desperately. "Just go ahead and tell us. It's Austin, isn't it?"

"Mr. and Mrs. Staley, we regret to have to tell you that your son, Austin, was killed in Iraq," the captain said, his voice low but firm. "He died in the line of duty. He was on a patrol west of Baghdad."

I stood staring at him, frozen in disbelief. No, not Austin. He couldn't be dead. Not Austin. I didn't cry. I gazed at the other soldier, a sergeant, who was standing behind the captain, his eyes on the floor. The captain, a tall, dark-haired man, placed a hand on Mom's shoulder, then turned and patted Dad's arm.

"If there is anything at all we can do, just let us know," he said.

"How did he die?" I asked. "Was it quick? Did he suffer?"

The two exchanged glances. Then the sergeant muttered, "It was an IED."

"A what?" I demanded. "Can you talk English?"

"I'm sorry," the captain injected. "It means an Improvised Explosive Device. The insurgents—the bad guys—hide them alongside the road, then set them off when our guys go by. Austin your brother?"

"Yes, he is," I said. And for the first time the tears began to flow, slowly at first, then a burst. I lost it. "Was it . . . was it quick?" I managed to say, sobbing.

"I'm sure . . . I'm sure it was pretty sudden," said the captain. "Why don't you sit down."

"I don't want to sit down." I stammered. "I want you—some-body—to tell me why my brother had to die. Why was he even over there?"

The captain turned to the sergeant, shrugging as he did. Then, "I'm sorry, young lady. I really am."

Mom's hysterical outburst had become more subdued, and was now a low sobbing. The sergeant and Dad helped her to the couch. Dad, meanwhile, stood silent, as though in shock. He just kept staring at a picture of Austin in his uniform.

The rest of the visit was surreal, like an old movie playing in the living room. My stomach felt hollow, and there was a ringing in my head.

The captain turned to me, "The Army will send a letter with more details. The body will be returned sometime within the next few days."

I stared at him. "He's not a body. He's my brother."

"I'm sorry," he said softly, fidgeting with his cap. "You know this is not easy for us. If there was any other way . . ." He shrugged.

I couldn't think about Christmas now, or anything else. My mind was a blank.

My dad saw the soldiers to the front door, sadly shaking hands with them. As he turned he looked gaunt, the eyes seemed sunken; there was an overall frail look about him. The sense of loss was like nothing I ever felt before. Austin was gone forever.

7

So Christmas 2004 was the worst one our family ever had. The big feast that evening never took place, and Mom went to lay down with a severe headache, all her hard work in the kitchen for nothing. Dad sat alone in the living room still staring at the framed photo of Austin.

I went in with Mom for a while, trying to comfort her as best I could. And then the friends and relatives, who had heard the news, began to come by. Mom was unable to deal with them, and it became my place to be the family greeter and spokesperson.

There would have been more, but since it was Christmas Eve most were at home celebrating the birth of Jesus Christ.

"Jesus," I said aloud, perhaps with some bitterness in my voice. "Where were you? Why were you not watching Austin? He was always true to you. I was always true to you."

Anger was mixing with grief.

We all had honestly believed Jesus would watch over him in Iraq. Austin had written that he believed he was being watched over. I went to my room then and stared at the picture of Jesus that sat on my dresser.

And then I turned it face down.

"If you were real, you would have watched over him," I said, the sound of my voice hollow and distant. "If you were as we believed, you'd have been there with him."

My eyes fastened for a moment on the pink angel. I shook my head, picked it up and tossed it into the trash basket. It was something that had been a part of me since I was a child. Now it no longer held any meaning.

I gazed up at the photo of Austin on the wall by the window. "Why did you have to go to Iraq anyway? You didn't have to die. You just had to go and volunteer. You should have been out in California or someplace safe."

Austin's funeral was to be four days later. He was flown by the military to Atlanta, and a hearse took the casket to a funeral home in Anniston. We couldn't open it, because of the severity of the wounds. And I didn't want to see him that way.

On the night he was there, I sat beside him until dawn, a hand on the casket.

Dad finally came back and told me to come home and rest.

The day of the funeral dawned cold and gray, and there were a few flakes of snow wafting about on a chill wind. The casket was taken to the Baptist church. The service passed in a blur. It all seemed distant, and I barely heard the words of the minister saying something about "he who believes in me can never die."

And my silent, cynical response was, "Yeah, right."

More accurate was the passage about a man being "like a flower . . . and soon cut down."

Mom and Dad were firm and erect, almost steely in their grief. I was all cried out; my eyes were dry and itchy. There was a mirror in the entrance of the church and I glanced at myself . . . the image looked hard and bitter. I didn't want to talk to anyone or to hear words meant to console me. There was an overwhelming urge to shout out at Mom and Dad that Austin had volunteered for Iraq. In a way, I was blaming him for his own death . . . and blaming his belief—and mine —in Jesus.

At the cemetery we sat on folding chairs under a green tent.

The wind hummed constantly and caused the flapping canvas to beat out a drum-like cadence. A line of grim-faced soldiers fired a salute. And then there came the sound of the bugle blowing "Taps," the wavering notes mingling with the cold breeze. I again wept for my brother. Mom and Dad broke down.

I hugged Mom as she embraced the American flag close to her chest. I decided not to ever tell her that her son volunteered to go to his death in some far-off hostile land . . . a place that I felt we did not belong.

And then it was over, and all that was left was the mound of flowers on his grave. We drove home in silence.

At the back door I paused before entering the house. Then I looked up at the hill. The brown grass was bending almost flat in the steady breeze that moaned over the barren land.

It was no longer like a sacred place. And I vowed that I would never go up there again.

8

New Year's passed without Dad watching any of the bowl games. In the past it seemed the world hinged on every play of every game. But this time, January 1, 2005, the TV set remained dead.

It was several days before I felt up to calling Ginger to see how she was doing and to report the bitter Christmas we had endured.

She seemed desperate to talk—who could blame her?—because hanging around a dormitory during the holidays can be a lonely thing, even more so for someone who is pregnant.

"Hey, roomie, happy holidays!" she cried, and I could almost see her beaming. "How ya doing?"

"Not well, Ginger," I said. "I didn't get a chance to call you, but my brother was killed in Iraq."

There was a brief silence, and I heard her sharp intake of air. "Oh, no. Wh— "

"The Army came to the door on Christmas Eve."

"When was he killed? How?"

"They said it was the just three days before Christmas." I groped for the right words. "They said it was some kind of . . . you know, some roadside bomb or something. The bad guys exploded it as he was walking by."

Again I heard the intake of air. "I'm so sorry."

"What about you?" I asked. "You decided anything about the . . . the baby?"

"Well, I had a scare when my parents said they would come up to visit me here," she said. "They couldn't understand why I couldn't come home for Christmas."

"Well, you could have come home with me," I said. "But as it turned out, it wouldn't have been much fun."

"It must have been awful."

"I wish you could have met Austin," I said. "He was a great brother."

"That would have been wonderful," she said. "Of course, he probably wouldn't want to be involved with someone like me."

"Certainly he would," I reassured her. "If he had met you, Ginger, he would have liked you. I told him about you. He was a great guy."

"I'll bet he was," she said. Then, "When are you coming back? Classes have started again."

"Don't know for sure." I tried to picture Ginger sitting there alone in our dorm room. "I would like to come back, but I don't think I can deal with school right now."

"One of your friends called," she said quickly. "You know, from the Christian group. I think he said his name was Glenn."

"Is that right?" I shrugged. "Glenn's an okay guy. But I think from now on my Tuesday nights will be free, Ginger. I'll be there to hang out with you. Maybe we can get a hobby."

"I still haven't decided what I'm going to do," she announced. "What do you think?"

What do you think? The words echoed in my head. I really didn't know what I thought anymore.

"What I think doesn't matter, Ginger," I said finally. "You have to go with what feels right for you. I know you heard a lot of preaching from me, but it's your life. You do what's best for you. After all, a baby might just strap you down."

There was a long pause as she absorbed the words. "You think it's okay to . . . you know . . . "

"Abortion, Ginger," I said. "You can say it."

"Well, I don't—what made you change your mind?"

"What changed me is what happened to my brother," I said. "I have no right to judge others and tell them what to do. We live for just a short time. So you have to make the best of it. Hauling a kid around doesn't sound like fun to me."

Ginger gave a bitter laugh. "Now I am confused. Do you think your mother would agree?"

"No, she wouldn't," I said quickly. "But it doesn't matter what my mother or your mother thinks. It's about you. It's your life, your body. But if you're going to go that route, you should do it soon. How far along are you?"

"Getting close to three months, I think." Then, wistfully, I heard her murmur, "I need to lean on someone." Then she hung up.

I winced. The call hadn't been much help to her. She sounded so desperate. One couldn't fully imagine what she might be going through.

The winter days passed so slowly then, and for our family it was like living in a world that was half-nightmare, half reality. My parents were almost like zombies. Mom spent much of her time battling headaches and staying in the bedroom. Dad went through the motions of trying to keep up with his insurance business, although he mostly sat in the living room.

One day the phone rang and after a brief conversation, Dad announced in a dull voice, "That was Jack Tolbert. He's not going to fool with soybeans this year."

So? Did it really matter if anyone rented twenty-five acres of our land? But Dad seemed interested in it. At least his mind was starting to think of other things besides Austin's death.

"Well, maybe someone else will want it," I said with a dis-interested shrug.

"He said he knew someone who was looking for some land to rent." Then he returned to his thoughts. I knew he was think-ing about Austin.

9

Several weeks had gone by since the funeral. Outside, the world had begun a subtle change: in the garden little tufts of green grass struggled into the cold sunlight; the forsythia bushes on the edge of the yard were starting to show swelling of the buds.

But it no longer seemed like a miracle to me as it did when I was growing up. It was just change. There was nothing divine about it.

The following Sunday morning I woke up early. It was still dark outside. The clock on the night stand read 5:30. Mom was clattering about in the kitchen; the aroma of coffee drifted through the house, beckoning me downstairs.

"Can't sleep?" she asked.

"I've been getting up early a lot lately," I said. "Just wake up. The other day it was three-thirty."

She nodded. "Me too. Your daddy's not been resting right, either. I worry about him."

But Mom seemed to be recovering slowly from Austin's death. At least she was starting to do things again, like cooking and dealing with the bills.

"Since you're up," she said, "we can get an early start for church."

"Church?" I hesitated, then said, "It doesn't start until nine."

"I know, but I mean we can start getting ready."

I had not been to services since Austin's funeral, making the excuse of not feeling well. It was going to be a problem telling her I no longer believed in the things that once guided my life and gave meaning to it.

Of course, she and Dad had been there every service, finding some strength in the togetherness of singing and praying.

But at some point she had to be told of my feelings. Maybe the time was now.

"Mom, I'm not ready to go back to church," I said softly. Then before she could reply, I added, "At least, not for awhile. You probably don't understand my feelings. It's hard to explain—"

"You're right, I don't understand," she shot back, giving me a brief, cold smile. The words had a testy edge to them. "Your daddy and I feel it's time for you to start going again." Then, in an accusing tone, she added, "You missed three Sundays in a row."

"Well, you and Dad go," I said, trying not to sound disrespectful. "I really don't feel up to it."

"Don't feel up to it," she said slowly, putting emphasis on each word. "Abbie, this is not like you."

"Mom, I'm eighteen. I think I can decide what I want to do."

"Oh, so now you're eighteen, and you make your own decisions?" She folded her arms and stared at me. "What has come over you?"

"You know what has happened. It was Austin." Then to try to change the subject I picked up a cup and went to the coffee maker. "Can I have some of this?"

"If Austin was standing right here," she snapped, "he would want you to go to church. And yes, you can have some coffee. You don't have to ask."

"Well, Austin is not here, and I'm not going." My voice had risen enough to wake Dad.

"Hey, what's going on down there?" he called.

"Nothing, Dad." I wished there was a place to hide. "We're talking about church."

With a look of disgust, Mom shouted, "It's about church, all right, only she doesn't want to go with us."

"What's that?" Now he was downstairs and stomping through the dining room, headed our way. "Doesn't want to go to church? Why? You sick?"

I shook my head and in my most patient voice declared, "I've been sick since Christmas Eve, Dad. I'm sorry, but I just don't want to go there anymore."

"She says it's because of Austin," Mom charged. "Blame Austin."

"Mom . . . no, I am not blaming Austin. It's just . . ." I couldn't go on with it and stalked out of the kitchen. "I'll be in my room."

"As long as you live under this roof," Dad called, "you'll abide by our wishes."

It didn't stop me. "I'm going to my room."

"Maybe that's a good place to be," he muttered angrily. Then to Mom, he said, "Don't worry yourself about it. It's just a phase or something."

10

Even with the coffee, I fell back asleep for a time, only to be awakened by the loud cawing of crows, who seemed to be in a shouting match. The house was quiet. Sunlight streamed in through the frosting of the side window of my room. Mom and Dad must have already gone to church.

I got up and glanced out at the side yard. It looked chilly. There was light frost coating the grass and on some of the brown leaves that clung to a white oak tree by the garage.

The back window of the room gave me a clear view of the garden and the hill. The drab, dark cherry trees seemed to glow in the sunlight. It was a quiet, peaceful morning. After being in the house for days, the outside seemed to invite me out just to breathe some fresh air.

I dressed in jeans and a heavy black-and-red plaid shirt that Austin used to wear. Mom had said something about giving his clothing away to a charity. I was against the idea. The shirt was a way of holding onto his memory.

Outside the crows kept up their incessant chatter, as though sounding an alarm. Of course, crows always sound that way. Austin used to say crows were his favorite birds, because they were so smart.

We had debated the issue several times. I personally liked cardinals and bluebirds the best. The thought of the exchanges about birds made me laugh. Then I realized that the thought

48

of the birds and Austin was the first time I had laughed since Christmas Eve.

I glanced down at the garden. The tomato vines were brittle and brown. Beside them was a square of corn stalks, which rattled like skeletons in the light wind. In years past, I would sometimes stand out there during the harvest season and watch the full moon rise. There was something about the pale light on the garden that gave me an eerie feeling. It was almost like a scene from a Disney Halloween tale.

My mind was dwelling on these things when, suddenly, I saw something move on the hill. It was by the cherry trees.

Was it the wind? Then I saw him, a man standing by the trees! For a moment a chill ran through my stomach. He was a stranger. My first thought was to run to the telephone and call 911.

And then I didn't see anything. He was gone! I blinked several times and focused my eyes on the trees. Yes, there he was again, standing in the sunlight, the breeze blowing his long brown hair. He was tall and lean and wore khaki pants and a blue, long-sleeved shirt.

It was disturbing to have a stranger on our land. I wished Dad and Mom were home. Maybe he was lost. At the very least he should be told he was on private land.

So I hurried downstairs and out the back door. Glancing up at the hill, I saw he was still there, seemingly just enjoying the warm sunshine. I moved toward the hill.

But before I could say anything, he called out quietly, "Good morning, Abbie."

The voice was low, quiet, and had a serene quality about it as it carried easily down the hillside. My mind raced to put a name to the voice. I couldn't.

As I watched him, he began to descend slowly. What was

he doing up there? And most importantly, how did he know my name?

"Are you well today?" he asked as he drew nearer.

"I'm okay." By instinct, I backed up a few steps. "Who are you?"

He eased closer, then answered, "A friend."

Now I could see his face more clearly. There was an inner voice telling me to run. I didn't know this man.

His features were finely chiseled, the skin smooth. The eyes were clear and brown and had a warm glow about them. He was not wearing shoes, but rather, leather sandals. He stopped about fifteen feet away, and regarded me with just a trace of a smile.

Oh, why didn't we have a big dog like other families?

"You know you're on private property," I said trying to sound firm but not hostile. And then a thought hit me. "Wait, are you the one who might rent the land for soybeans?"

He gave a slight shrug and smiled. Then he gestured toward the hill, "So that's your sacred ground up there?"

Who told him that? Could he have known Austin?

"It's just a hill," I said, still studying him.

"How's the Cutlass running?" he asked.

"It's—it's running," I stammered, surprised by the question. How did he know about my car? "Do you know my dad?"

"It is such a nice day," he said, ignoring the question. "I thought I would drop by and say hello." Then he raised his right hand. "It was nice to talk with you again, Abbie. Drive careful going back to school."

And with that he turned and strode up the hill at a brisk, but effortless gait. I started to call after him, to know who he was. But he was soon over the incline and out of sight.

I felt an impulse to run after him to see where he was going. But my feet were frozen to the ground. This just couldn't end this way. Despite the pledge made after Austin's funeral, I broke into a run, and rushed up the slope.

At the top I stopped and glanced hurriedly about. He was gone! There was nothing below but open fields and pasture. Where could he be? There was no place to hide. For fully five minutes I looked about, straining my eyes for sight of him. But he had vanished.

Confused and a little frightened, I retraced my steps to the house, went to the kitchen and poured another cup of coffee. My hands were shaking.

What a strange visit . . . and did it really happen? Did I really see somebody out there? Maybe my mind was overworked from the stress of Austin's death, I thought. How could somebody know so much about me? About the hill? That I drove a clunker, or went to college?

11

A short time later my parents returned home. I could tell Mom was still sore at me, and Dad didn't seem to be in a much better mood.

"Thought you'd be asleep yet," he called. The tone was tinged with annoyance.

"Sorry I upset you," I said. "I didn't mean to."

"Well, you did upset us," Mom said, hanging up her coat. "And you missed a good sermon, too. It was about having faith. You could have learned something."

I started to tell them about the visitor, but then decided against it. Maybe it was not a good time. But I did ask, "Has anyone said anything about renting the soybean field?"

Dad gave me a puzzled glance. "No, why?"

"Just wondered. How about the car? You said anything to anyone about looking at it? A mechanic, I mean?"

"The car? You mean the Cutlass?"

"Yeah. My car, Dad, that green thing out there."

"No, haven't had time to think about it," he said. "Why these questions?"

"Nothing. I just wondered."

Well, that sure didn't clear anything up for me, I thought. It just seemed to muddle the picture more. So he wasn't a farmer, and he wasn't a mechanic.

Mom went into the kitchen to prepare dinner. Over her

shoulder, she called, "You going back to school today?" She still sounded disappointed in me.

"Yeah, I guess," I said without much enthusiasm. "It's time to try to get back to normal again."

"Yes it is," she said, turning to face me, "and normal means going back to church, too, young lady."

She didn't miss a chance, I thought, but I did not venture a reply.

Instead, I asked, "Have you ever noticed a man around here with sort of long brown hair . . . well, have you ever seen him?"

"Long hair?" Dad growled, glancing at me. "How long? Did he have a beard?"

"A beard?" I puzzled. "Gee, I really didn't notice. I guess maybe he did. He was sort of young, but not real."

Now Dad studied me more intently. "You see somebody that looked like that?"

I fibbed. "From the window. He was out by the road."

Then Dad chuckled. "I haven't seen anyone like that, and don't want to."

Coming out of the kitchen, Mom heard the comment. "Was he hanging around here? Maybe he's some kind of poet or something. You know they look like that, some of them."

"Yeah, like those old beatniks we read about," Dad said. Both of them smiled

It was good to see some cheer in them, after the long period of mourning—and their anger at me. But I didn't laugh. I just stared at them, wondering.

12

After dinner, I packed up my things and loaded them into the car. It was time to try to get back to my life again. But it was to be different, I felt. Dad told me to be careful driving, and watch for state troopers. Mom eased up about church, and gave me a hug, plus a sack full of cooked food.

"Now you tell Ginger to take care of herself," she said. "And you can bring her home anytime you want. You don't have to call and ask or anything."

"What's wrong with Ginger?" Dad asked.

"Nothing," I said, glancing quickly at Mom. She couldn't have leaked our secret, could she? "Why?"

"Well, your mother said for her to take care of herself," he said. "I just wondered if there was something wrong with her."

"Oh, no, nothing wrong with her," Mom added hastily to squelch any hint of trouble. "It's just something I say."

Then I started up the motor. I hadn't driven it since arriving home on Christmas Eve. I almost fainted. It sounded like a new car. I heard Dad call out in surprise.

I rolled the window down. "You hear that?"

He nodded emphatically. "I told you there wasn't a thing wrong with it."

"Well, it didn't sound like this when I came home," I said, mystified. "It sounds great."

"Be careful," Mom called.

Driving off, it occurred to me that Dad must have found

time to have someone fix whatever was wrong with the Cutlass. I made it to Birmingham by the middle of the afternoon. It was strange being back at the dorm, as though I had been gone for years. I felt older somehow, and different. Maybe it was because things *were* different.

Opening the door to the room, I was greeted with a squeal of delight from Ginger. She ran to me arms outstretched. "You're back!" she cried. "For gosh sakes I'm so happy."

I struggled in with my suitcase and removed a plate of chicken and apple pie from the sack. "Here. Mom sent this for you. She wants you to eat properly."

"All right!" she cried eagerly. "This is on target. I'm starved."

I sat down on the bed beside her. "So, what have you been doing? Living on fast food?"

"No, I cooked some veggies now and then." She gobbled down a chicken wing. "Your friend from the group called again. I told him I didn't know when you might be back. What's his name? Glenn something."

"Glenn Lyons."

"That's it. Sounds like a nice guy."

"Yeah, I guess. So, what have you decided?"

She stopped eating, and looked at me. "About the baby?"

"Well . . . yes, about the baby," I said, smiling at her drift from reality. "What else do you have to decide about?"

She stuffed the last of the pie into her mouth. "Don't know yet."

I stood and paced about the room. "You know, I told you from the first about how things should be done. Well, you know, I was probably preaching."

"You were!" she gushed, smiling at me. "You were preaching, all right, lady."

"Well, as I told you on the phone, I had no right to," I said, still serious. "This is your life, and you should decide what you're going to do about . . . about things."

Now her face clouded. "Why are you telling me this? You told me you had changed because of what happened to your brother."

"Yes, I've changed," I said. "You know, it seems like a lot of my life has been wasted on something that doesn't exist. I've lost what faith I had, or whatever you want to call it. We're alone here, Ginger, and we have to decide what's best."

"Alone?" she asked. "You mean alone in the world?"

"I mean alone on this Earth," I said sternly. "There's nothing or nobody else out there. You were right all along. I was wrong."

Ginger stood up and went to the sink, rinsing her hands. She didn't look at me.

"You're the one who told me to do what was right," she said finally, glancing over her shoulder at me. "All that stuff about prayers and all."

"I know. But it's still going to be all right," I said. "You know, the world's not going to end today or anything."

Then she turned and gazed at me. "Do you think I still need to keep the baby—or what?"

"Well, I—that's up to you. That's your choice. But either way, I'll stick by you. You're my best friend. Okay?"

She smiled. Then, in a cheerless voice, she said, "Times two."

That evening Glenn Lyons called me. "Glad you're back," he said. "Just wanted to remind you about Tuesday evening. We're planning to—"

"Can't make it, Glenn," I interrupted.

You could feel the surprise at the other end of the line. "Can't make it? Well, okay, then I guess we'll see you next Tuesday."

"Don't think so, Glenn," I said. "I don't mean to sound like a jerk, but I'm not coming back to the group. It's nothing personal, or anything. I'm just not."

"Something wrong?"

"Well, it's just that I have a lot of work to catch up. And—"

"Your roommate told me about your brother," he said. "I'm so sorry."

"Yeah, well, we just have to deal with it. Things change. People change."

"So you're not coming back at all?" he asked, his voice reflecting disappointment.

"That's what I have decided," I said. "To be blunt about it, I just don't have any feelings about religion anymore."

He didn't respond at first. Then he said, "Well, I'm sorry you feel that way."

"It's not your fault," I said. "It's just something that happened."

"Yeah, we were looking forward to having you with us Thursday. We're planning a prayer vigil at one of the clinics."

"Well, that's something that should be left up to a woman," I said. "Actually, I couldn't care less about it."

There was the moment of shocked silence. Then Glenn said, "Maybe we'll see each other one day."

"That would be nice," I said. "Bye, Glenn."

13

A nd so I made it official—I was no longer Baptist or a Christian, not a disciple of anything. Of course, I wouldn't get in the way of other people who wanted to believe what they chose, be they Christian, Jew, Muslim or whatever. Now Ginger and I were on the same playing field, two non-believers. I could concentrate on studies. And I could concern myself with my friend. Her problems became my problems by virtue of our friendship. If I could help, I would. On Tuesday nights when I would have been meeting with the Christian group I could now be with her.

We took advantage of the free time. One Tuesday night we went to a movie, another one we went out and splurged on an expensive meal, which neither of us could afford. But it was something to do.

Meantime, I had reenrolled in classes, repeatedly being told I had much catching up to do. I could do it.

One cold night in late February I was sleeping soundly when Ginger shook me awake, jabbering excitedly about something.

"What's wrong?" I muttered, rubbing my eyes.

"Nothing," she said. "I just decided what I'm going to do."

"You did what?"

"I'm keeping the baby," she cried. "Aren't you glad?"

I yawned and sat up. "Well . . . yes, real glad. How did you decide that?"

Ginger gave me a brief smile and shook her head. "You believe in dreams?"

Dreams? I shrugged. "The kind you think about or the ones that come when you're sleeping?"

"Sleeping," she murmured. "I just dreamed that I had the baby and some man was handing it to me. Real strange. I take that as a sign."

Now fully awake, I asked, "You going to keep the baby yourself?"

She nodded happily. "Yeah. You want some ice cream?"

"Ice cream? Now? What time is it?"

"Who cares what time it is? Here, I'll get you a bowl."

So we ate ice cream at zero-dark-thirty, and talked about the coming event of a birth.

"Well, we'll have to move out of the dorm," I said. "Maybe we can get an apartment that's not too expensive. I can get a job and help you with the baby."

"You will? Help me, I mean?"

"Of course. What are best friends for?"

"You'll probably have to drive me to the hospital, you know." Then she laughed. "Hope that old green car will make it."

Her words suddenly rang a bell with me. That old green car. Why was it running so well?

"Something wrong?" she asked, the smile fading.

"No, nothing wrong." I put the bowl in the sink. "I was just thinking about the car. You know, something strange happened when I was home."

"Strange? What happened?"

"There was a man up on that hill behind our house."

"Yeah? Who was it? What happened that's so strange?"

I turned to her. "I don't know. I'm not a hundred percent sure I saw him—or talked to him, for that matter. He was . . . I can't explain it. He was just there. And he walked away over the hill, so I ran to see where he had gone. And when I got to the top he was gone. I mean it was like he flat vanished."

Ginger had stopped eating and her eyes were riveted on me. "That's not just strange," she said softly. "That's almost . . . well, like something supernatural."

"What?" I said, fixing a look of mock anger at her. "You're the one who never believed in stuff like that."

She gave me a sheepish grin. "I guess deep down I do. I just never went to church or anything. I mean I did when I was little, but I quit when I came here."

"Yeah, well, eat up," I said. "I'm going back to sleep. We can talk more tomorrow."

Before I could get under the covers, she called, "What did the man look like?"

I paused, then propping on an elbow, turned to look at her. "Why? What did the man in the dream look like?"

She stared up at the ceiling. "I couldn't see clearly. Just a man. Middle-aged, maybe. But he had long hair. Brown, I think."

I felt a jump-start in my chest. Long brown hair. "Ginger," I said, "you believe in dreams. Do you also believe in coincidence?"

"What?" she asked as she got into her bed. "Your guy have long brown hair, too?"

"I think so," I said. Then, "I think you made a wise decision."

"Me too," she said eagerly.

14

The next afternoon, after classes, we met at a coffeehouse near the campus. Both of us had ideas about the future we faced, with a baby entering her life and mine.

She had picked up a copy of a community newspaper and had already marked some apartments for rent. Most sounded too expensive.

"What about jobs?" I asked.

"Well, I didn't look, but there must be some in here."

We drank coffee and talked for an hour or so, then came to a joint conclusion. Ginger just had to tell her parents what was going on.

"They'll kill me," she said.

"No they won't," I said. "I'll be with you. How far is it down there?"

"About two hundred miles. It's about a hundred miles below Montgomery."

We decided to go the next morning, skipping classes for a day.

Ginger's parents both worked, she told me as we drove south on Interstate 65 that next morning. Her mother owned a floral shop which kept her quite busy, and her father was a banker who drove a few miles to the town of Ozark, which was near Fort Rucker, the Army helicopter training center.

We arrived early in the afternoon. The house was outside of the small community of Howton Crossroads, and at first glance

I wondered how her mother's flower shop could stay afloat financially. The house was brick, and sat on a five-acre plot. The nearest neighbor was about a half mile away.

"Is anyone home?" I asked, as we got out of the car.

"I got a key," she said, her voice tense.

"Now don't be so worried," I scolded softly. "It'll be all right."

We entered the house and Ginger got the telephone. I waited nearby, watching her as she dialed.

"Mom? It's me. I'm home." There was a pause, while her mother responded to the surprise visit. Then after a minute or so, Ginger said, "Well, I know this is a busy time, Mom. But can't you come home for a couple of minutes? I need to talk to you."

Then she put the phone down, staring at it a moment and biting her lip.

"Maybe we should have called first," I said.

Ginger nodded. "Maybe. She said she was really busy. I guess we could have gone by there."

About fifteen minutes later we heard a car door slam, followed shortly by someone turning the door knob. I felt a tightness in my stomach. There was no way to know what to expect for sure.

The door opened and a petite woman with reddish-brown hair entered; she appeared much younger than I had expected.

She stopped as she entered the living room. Ginger did not get up from the couch. I stood.

"Well, hello," she said. "You must be Abbie."

"Yes, ma'am."

Then she turned to Ginger, leaned over and gave her a hug. "Darling, I see you have changed a bit." The words were frosty.

"Hi, Mom," Ginger said softly. "Sorry you had to learn this

way. I was scared to tell you. I'm sorry."

I decided it was time for the two to talk without me. "Excuse me, but I'm going to get a drink of water." Ginger shot an accusing look at me, as though I was bailing out, leaving her stranded.

Staying in the kitchen kept me out of earshot. But after a few minutes Mrs. Burns called me to come back. Ginger stared at the floor.

"Are you girls hungry?" Mrs. Burns asked.

We both said no, but she ignored it and fixed sandwiches anyway. I noted that Ginger had been crying, and her mother seemed to have some eye trouble, too.

"So I hear you two are thinking of finding an apartment and rooming together for awhile longer," Mrs. Burns said, fighting to control her voice. She was looking at me as she spoke.

"That's the plan, yes, ma'am."

"Well, I hope it works out as planned," she said tersely.

We ate in silence for the most part, and then Mrs. Burns called her husband. I now understood Ginger's anxiety about coming home. The tension was so thick you almost had to elbow your way through.

Then Mr. Burns arrived. He was a dapper looking man in a blue suit. He too looked a bit younger than I expected. He gave a cool nod at me and shook hands, and then glanced at his daughter.

"So you were too busy to come home for Christmas," he said, without touching her. Instead he took a seat in the corner, his eyes shifting quickly from Ginger to the floor.

"Yeah," she said. "I guess I was."

I clenched my teeth to keep quiet. His words were cruel, cutting. It occurred to me that our family was quite happy. My thoughts escaped to that afternoon of Christmas Eve when my father entered the kitchen talking about the aroma of good food and eagerly rubbing his stomach. It made me smile. Then I was pulled back to the Burns' living room.

"Well, I'll tell you my thoughts," Ginger's father said. "I'm not happy the way things are going, but it's too late to change course. And it's going to be our grandchild, and we'll help. But you got yourself into this and you'll have to deal with it. Your mother and I will help with the medical costs and we will pay half the rent and utilities once you find a place. And we'll get through this, we'll get through this—somehow."

And with that he arose, nodded at me, and then headed for the front door, without even a glance at his distressed daughter. He left, pulling the door closed behind him.

Well, I thought, it could have been worse. And it wasn't such a bad deal. We could come up with half the costs of an apartment.

But before I could say anything, the door opened again and Mr. Burns strode back in, went to Ginger, bent over and kissed her on the head. Then he left.

Afterwards, she turned to me, laughed slightly as she blinked back some tears, and said, "Well, buddy, you ready to hit the road?"

Standing, I said, "It wasn't so bad, did you think? Your dad is okay."

"He can be a jerk!" Mrs. Burns called from the kitchen. "But we can deal with him."

She packed some sandwiches and cookies, then bade us good-bye, thrusting a couple of twenty-dollar bills in my hand. "That's for gasoline," she said.

Then we left. Ginger looked lighter and her face was aglow.

15

By now it was mid-March and the days began to lengthen and mellow. The wisteria and forsythia were out in brilliant yellows and reds. The daffodils had already bloomed.

One Saturday morning I awoke to see the sun splashing a yellow glow on the wall. I rose up on one elbow and threw a pillow at Ginger, who was sleeping away with her head covered with blankets. "Hey, you sorry thing," I said. "Let's get up and do something today. Come on, you old grandma."

She groaned. "Why don't you go back where you came from?"

"Come on. Get up."

I got up and made coffee. Then Ginger struggled to a sitting position. "Hey, that smells good," she muttered.

After pouring a cup, I sat at the little kitchen table. "Help yourself."

As she lumbered to the table, I glanced at her. She was really starting to get large. She was probably past the halfway point of her pregnancy.

"What is it that you want to do?" she asked.

"I don't know," I said. "Let's just get out of this place. It's so nice out. The sun's shining, the flowers are out."

"You forgot about birds singing," she said sarcastically. Then she gave me a wan smile. "Yeah, the flowers are out, and I'm like the last rose of summer."

We ate cereal, washed up, got dressed and headed out. It was already late morning. A lot of people had the same idea we did. They just wanted to get out and enjoy the spring-like air.

There was a mini-park about three blocks away, and we headed in that direction.

It was already crowded when we arrived. Children were on the swings, and a barbecue stand had been set up near the center of the green.

"Let's find a bench where we can crash," Ginger pleaded.

"Okay, okay," I said. "Are you all right?"

"Yeah, just tuckered out from that short walk."

"You need a drink . . . a soda or orange drink?"

She nodded. "Do you mind? Maybe a 7-Up or Sprite."

I went to the barbecue stand where a long line had already formed. This was going to be great, I thought. It could take fifteen minutes to get waited on.

Than a voice behind me said, "How's your friend doing?"

I whirled around. It was him! It was the man that I saw that day on the hill! A warning bell went off in my brain.

"What are you doing here?" I asked.

He smiled. "Standing in line. How are you, Abbie?"

I didn't want to make a scene. But I was concerned about him showing up where I was.

"How'd you know I'd be here?"

"I just knew. I know a lot of things." And then he held up something. "I believe this is yours."

My stomach went cold. It was the pink angel!

"Where did you get that?" I demanded. "How? I can't believe this."

"I know about you," he said, his voice remaining at a low

pitch. And then he said, "I know about Austin."

"Austin? You know Austin?" I was astounded by his words. How did he know?

And then I drew the angel near to my chest. Almost pleading, I asked, "Who are you?"

"I said I was a friend. You knew me once, Abbie."

If there was a place to run, I would have. I was scared. This wasn't real!

"When did I know you?" I cried.

"All your life," he replied, that same quiet smile lighting his face.

"Austin? How do you know my brother?"

"He called on me," he said quietly. "He is with me now. I wanted to tell you that."

"What are you saying?" Looking about quickly to make sure I wasn't being overheard, I pursued in a near whisper, "Are you telling me you're Christ? Is that what you're saying?"

He looked into my eyes, into my soul. Now the smile faded. He nodded.

"Why do you expect me to believe that?" I asked. "Am I going crazy? The other time you just—just disappeared."

He shook his head slowly. "Abbie, you do not need a miracle to believe."

My hands were shaking . . . I couldn't believe this. Here he was in front of me, and I was not sure. I was doubting. But how could I be sure?

"Hey, let's move the line, lady," a man in back called.

I edged backward, my eyes still on him. "Why should I believe this?"

He slowly reached out and took my hand—it was like electricity ran through me, pulsating, yet not causing pain. I could only look into his eyes. I can't explain the feeling, but in that moment I knew then that it was Him. Then he let go of my hand. He smiled.

"You say you lost your faith," he said. "But you never did. I knew you never would. And now you are taking care of a friend who needs help."

With that he glanced over toward the bench where Ginger was waiting.

"There is no greater faith than helping one in need. A girl who believes angels put blossoms on trees could never leave a friend to face a storm alone."

I dropped my eyes, unable to look at him. He knew so much. "What do you want of me?"

"I just came to see you because you were so troubled," he said.

"You came to see me?"

"Yes. Is that all right with you?"

"Yes, yes. I—I just can't believe it." I stammered. "I mean it's hard to believe you came to see me."

The man in back of the line was getting highly disturbed. "Hey, how about moving the line!"

"You hear the man back there?" my friend asked. "He's real and I'm real."

I felt light, bubbly all over. This could not be happening.

The line edged forward and I turned around to move ahead. As I pivoted again to face him, I saw the loudmouth from the back. He was a husky man, heavyset, with close-cropped reddish hair. He was coming forward, apparently to complain about how slow the line was moving. He looked like he had been drinking. He had a cup from a fast-food restaurant in his hands.

He stopped and looked down at the sandals of my friend. "Who you supposed to be?" he sneered. "Jesus Christ?"

If he only knew, I thought.

But Jesus smiled at him. "I think you need another drink of water."

"What?"

"Have another drink of your water, my friend."

The man put the cup to his mouth and took a swallow. "Hey!" he yelled, "what'd you do to my drink? This is nothing but water!"

With that the man began to back away, his eyes on us. "Hey!" he shouted. "Hey! He turned vodka into water! He did it! I think it's Jesus! I think it's Jesus!"

I looked up at my friend. He smiled. "I think it's time for me to take my leave."

"You're leaving? I—you said you were with Austin? Is he okay?"

"He's fine."

Now the people were gathering closer, staring. The man was pointing at us and yelling that he had seen Jesus. That's when two police officers came and took him by the arm.

"Austin's okay?" I asked again. "Can I ever see him? Please?"

He nodded. "One day you will."

"I mean now," I said hesitantly. "Can we do that?"

He gazed into my eyes for a moment. Then he said, "You will see him. Soon."

"There are so many things I want to ask you," I said, keeping my voice low. "Do you come here often? I mean to this world."

"Sometimes. I have been to a few places. Nobody recognized me." He smiled at that.

Out of the corner of my eye I saw Ginger coming toward me, and right behind her was another police officer. Things were getting out of hand.

"Abbie," she called, "you okay? What's going on?"

I looked at her for a moment. "It's all right. Just a drunk came by. He's out of it."

"What was he saying about Jesus?" she asked.

"Well, he was—"

I looked and he was gone! My eyes darted over the area. No sign of him. Suddenly, I was frantic. How could he be gone so quickly?

"Ginger, did you see him? Where did he go?"

"Who? The man you were talking to?"

"Yes! Yes! Did you see?"

"I don't know," she cried. "Who is he?'

A dark-haired woman behind me, wearing an orange sweater and faded blue jeans, stared at me with a perplexed expression.

"Where did he go?" she said, a smile of awe breaking across her face. "I saw him talking to you. And I looked over at the police and then I looked back and he was gone."

Ginger was staring at me. "Who was it?" she asked.

I took her arm. "Come on, Ginger. Let's get you that Sprite. We'll talk later."

"Did he just leave?" she asked. "And you look like you've seen . . . a ghost or something, I don't know what. Who was he?"

"A friend," I said, my voice seemingly far away. I felt a strange sensation over my entire body, a feeling I could never explain.

By now we were at the front of the line. I took the drink with quivering hands. Then we started back to the bench. I felt I was walking on clouds. People were staring at us.

"That was just a friend," I repeated. "Just an old friend. And I can't believe I saw him. I can't believe it."

"Well, gee whiz, he looked like a big brother or something," Ginger said. "How old is he?"

"You know what? I'd guess that he must be about thirty-three or so." I said vaguely. "But he's a real friend. You'd like him, Ginger. You really would."

"Some friend," she muttered. "Just literally disappears."

She started to sit down at the bench, but I waved her forward. "Come on, let's go back to our room. I'm kinda tired."

Some of the park visitors were pointing at me. When we reached the street a police car pulled up. I heard the drunk calling out again as officers led him out of the park in handcuffs . . .

"There she is," he cried, using an elbow to point at me. "That blonde there, she was the one he was talking with. I saw them. It was Jesus Christ, I swear it was."

"All right, so you saw Jesus," one of the escorting officers said. "Get in the car. Watch your head."

The man was still looking at me, "I'm gonna quit drinking. And I'm going to church."

Ginger tapped me on the shoulder. "You gonna tell me what's going on? One minute we're minding our own business in a park, next thing I see this . . . this person talking with you and then the police come."

Before I could say anything one of the officers, an African American, came over. He grinned. "Look, you haven't done anything. But what in the world is this guy talking about?"

"He just started yelling that he saw Jesus," I said. "Has he been drinking?"

"Yeah, that's what he keeps saying," the officer said.

Then he looked off past me, thinking. "I know he was drinking. He keeps telling us he had vodka and some kind of soda in the container. But when we checked it we found nothing but plain water."

"What's going to happen to him?" I asked.

"Oh, he'll go to jail for a day or so," the officer replied.

I felt some blame for the man's arrest. "Could you just drive him home?"

"Drive him home?" The officer shrugged. "Probably not. He seems to have got quite a shock. Either way, we'll have to make a report. We already radioed in that there was a disturbance."

Ginger tugged at my arm. "Can we leave? I'm getting tired."

The officer hesitated, looking down at the grass. His expression told me he wanted to get more answers. But then he shook his head and said, "Y'all have a good day."

They left then. And we walked to the dorm.

16

Back at the room I sat in the kitchen, sipping a glass of lemonade, and thinking about the visit. I still felt like I could walk on air. Ginger was behind me heating up a can of tomato soup.

"So, did your friend bring you that pink angel?" she asked.

"What? Oh, that. Yeah, yeah, he did."

She came to the table and picked it up, examining it. "Didn't you once tell me you had one like this at home in your room?"

"I think I did tell you that. It was lost. He just gave me one back."

She looked at it more closely. "This one doesn't look new."

"No, it probably isn't. It's like the original."

"Looks to me like it could be the one you had before."

"I don't know where he got it," I said. And that was the truth.

Then she fixed a suspicious gaze on me. "Thought you were finished with religion and all that. You said you had wasted much of your life."

Well, she had me there. Those were my words, all right.

"Maybe I was confused," I said finally. "Nobody's perfect. You know like that Simon and Garfunkel song, 'sometimes I'm mistaken, sometimes confused, and certainly misused,' or whatever. You remember that? That might be the case."

"Oh, so that's the case."

Then she became dead serious. "Who was your friend?"

"I told you. Just a friend."

"Doesn't have a name, Miss Staley?" she inquired, doing her best Matlock impression. "Where did he go? And why was that man saying it was Jesus?"

I shook my head, which still felt light and almost floating away. "Ginger, if I told you, you would never believe it."

"Try me."

"Well, all right, but don't go into labor or anything, okay? You remember me telling you about the man on the hill?"

"Yeah, I don't remember the Simon and Garfunkel song," she said, grinning, "but I remember about the man on the hill."

"This was him again," I said, standing up and pacing about. "And it was . . . it was Jesus."

At that she sat up straighter at the table, her eyes narrowed. "You're telling me it was Jesus Christ? The Jesus Christ?"

"Yes, I'm telling you that," I said. "He came down here, that's the truth. He told me about Austin. He knew! And the angel? I threw it into the trash, Ginger. But he found it. He found it. So he talked about faith. It was only for a minute or two at most. And then he just—he just vanished into thin air. That's why the drunk guy kind of went wacky. And the woman behind me looked like her eyes were going to pop out. She could hardly speak. And I don't know where he went. Just vanished."

Ginger had her chin propped on a hand as she listened. She said not a word. Then she began sipping the tomato soup.

"Well, you've nothing to say?" I asked. "You're just going to eat tomato soup?"

"I caught just a glimpse of him," she said softly.

"Look, I don't know why he chose me to visit, I really don't," I said, almost defensive about it. "But you saw him, too? That makes me feel better. At least I wasn't seeing things."

"You certainly were not seeing things," Ginger agreed. "Somebody was there. He looked like the paintings I've seen. He really did. But I can't say it was Jesus Christ. And how do you know it was really him?"

I threw my arms out in a hopeless gesture. "I don't know how to do anything."

"Is he coming back?'

Coming back. I thought about it for an instant.

"Yes he is!" I said excitedly. "He said he would bring my brother for me to see. He said that."

"When?"

"Don't know. He just said it."

"Did he say where? Like in the park, or what?"

"No, but he said it," I cried. "But he didn't say when or where."

For a long time neither of us said anything. Ginger finished her soup, and I finally drank the lemonade.

Then she grinned, the kind of grin a child shows when she or he is getting into mischief. "Can I call the *National Enquirer*?" she teased. She laughed. "I'm only kidding. I wouldn't do that. But somebody might. Lot of people there today."

I sat down again, thinking. "You're right. Somebody probably will call them or the local TV stations. Or the newspapers. Good Lord. The officer said they would make a report. I think the *Birmingham News* runs brief listings of police reports."

"They do," she said. "And if they see that someone thought they saw Jesus, it will more than likely end up in the paper."

"Well," I said, "he didn't say to keep things quiet. But I just assumed it was a private visit. I don't know. People don't know who I am, except for the drunk, and maybe that officer."

"That could be two people too many," Ginger said slowly.

17

The following Monday we returned to class and life seemed to be back to normal. My last class was in the early afternoon and afterwards I was walking back to the dorm, deep in thought. Then I heard someone call, "Hey, Abbie." I turned and saw Glenn Lyons hurrying my way.

I turned and waited for him. "Hey, what's happening?"

"You see today's paper?" he asked, a smile lighting up his face.

I blinked several times in dreadful surprise. "The paper? No, why?"

"They had a little story about some guy arrested here on campus Saturday," he said. Then he adjusted his glasses. "Claimed he saw Jesus. Crazy, isn't it?"

"Oh, yeah, crazy," I said, trying to cover the uneasy wave that swept over me. "I'll see if there's a paper at the dorm."

He looked at me closely. "You okay?"

"Yeah, I'm fine. I just gotta get back to the room. There's a lot of stuff to do."

"Oh, okay. Your roommate all right?"

"Ginger? Oh, yeah. She's fine."

"She sounds nice," he said. "I talked to her a few times on the phone."

"I know. She told me. Talk to you later, Glenn."

"All right. I'll call you guys sometime."

With a wave of my hand, I turned and resumed my walk to the dorm. It was in the newspaper! I rushed into the lobby, checking the coffee tables. Somebody usually left a copy scattered around. But there wasn't one in sight. I ignored the elevator and ran up the stairs.

Opening the door, I rushed in, breathing hard. Ginger was sitting on her bed. She immediately jumped up.

"Hey, is this an invasion?" She grinned as she held up the newspaper. "You gotta look at this."

I grabbed it from her. There on the upper lefthand corner was a short story. It read:

Man Says Jesus
At UAB Campus

UAB police arrested a man Saturday who claims he saw Jesus Christ at a park outing. Harvey Ballard, 24, was charged with public intoxication. The police report says Ballard, who is not a student, claimed the man he said was Jesus was talking with a young woman. Ballard told officers the man altered his alcoholic drink to plain water, then vanished. The name of the young woman was omitted from the report. Aaron Brown, a UAB spokesman, said there was a disturbance reported and campus police responded. He said he did not know the name of the young woman and was not sure she was a student.

I tossed the paper on the table. "They don't know who we are. They're not even sure I'm a student. That's good."

"Hey, we're not fugitives or anything," Ginger said. "I told you I should have called the *Enquirer*."

"I don't really care about newspaper stories," I said.

My thoughts were on the pending miracle that was going to take place. Jesus said he was going to bring my brother back so I could see him. Nothing like that ever happened in the Bible that I knew of, although I was hardly a student of scripture.

But when and where was the question. Everything had happened so fast at the park that I hadn't asked him.

That night I was trying to do some reading and some written work that had to be turned in by week's end, when the telephone rang. Ginger picked it up.

"It's Glenn," she said in a stage whisper. Then, she put the phone to her ear. In an above-normal pitch, she said, "Oh, really? It was? Tonight? Okay, let me tell her."

I glanced up expectantly, waiting for whatever the message might be.

Still holding the phone, Ginger announced, "The story about Jesus was on the television news tonight. Glenn says they interviewed the man who was arrested. And he said he saw Jesus talking with a girl with a long blonde ponytail."

She resumed the conversation. I felt the butterflies in my stomach again. Then I heard Ginger relay, "What? Oh, yeah, it does sort of sound like Abbie, all right. She's blonde." She rolled her eyes and shrugged. "What? Oh, no, I haven't heard her say a word about anything like that."

So it was getting uncomfortable, with the story leaking out. If Glenn was thinking it might have been me, then there might be others. And what about the guy who had been arrested? Would he come looking for me later? I thought about people stalking me to try to get a photograph; of endless phone calls; reporters showing up at the front door; television crews prowling the hallways trying to film me in class. And the tabloids . . . Lord, I could see the headlines now: The girl who talked with Jesus.

It would be like the people who saw flying saucers, I thought.

The news people always made fun of those who lived in mobile homes. What would they do with a girl from rural Alabama?

It didn't matter. What I saw was real; what I saw was the truth.

18

By mid-April the weather was melting into warm days, and some of them were actually hot. Classes were winding down as we headed toward final exams.

I had started wearing sunglasses and a baseball cap. It helped me deal with the growing heat, but also served as a way of hiding my identity. In fact, Ginger and I celebrated my nineteenth birthday at an Italian restaurant, and I kept the sunglasses on even though it was dark.

But all the while I kept thinking of him. Where would his return take place? Would he just come to the dorm? No, I thought, he wouldn't do something to panic a bunch of young women.

Ginger, to my surprise, came up with a great idea.

"Why don't we go back to the park?" she suggested. "That's where he was before. Maybe that's where he will show up again."

So that afternoon after we had finished classes, we strolled back to the park. I had the cap pulled down low. We walked by it at first and glanced casually. There were only a few people sitting on the benches, or walking slowly through the fresh green grass.

"Looks quiet," I said. "You want to just sit down over there?"

"Sounds good," she said. "I'm getting worn out anyway."

We sat for a time, saying nothing. Then I opened a book

and pretended to read. Every so often I would cast a sweeping glance over the area. There was no sign of him.

A half-hour passed. Nothing. Then Ginger cleared her throat, turned to me, and said, "Look, Abbie, don't be disappointed if he doesn't show."

"I'm not disappointed," I said. "There's no way of knowing."

"Well, it was a long shot, you have to admit."

"Yeah, it was that, all right," I said, with a sigh. "A long shot."

"You think we should head back?" Ginger said. "Mosquitoes are starting to come out."

I closed the book. "Whatever you want to do."

We started to get up. Then Ginger groaned, "Oh, no. Not him."

I followed her gaze to the middle of the park. There walking toward us was the stout, red-haired man who had been arrested that day.

"Just be cool," I cautioned. "Sit still."

He walked closer, his head lowered like a bull as he peered at us. He stopped about ten feet away.

"Is that you?" he called. The voice was surprisingly polite.

We glanced at each other. Then Ginger said, "You talking to us?"

"I was talking to your friend there," he said. "Aren't you the one he was speaking with that day?"

"What do you mean?" I said, glancing about in hopes a police officer might be in sight. But there was no such luck.

"I know it's you," he said. "Because you were with the pregnant girl that day. And that's her sitting right there with you."

How stupid of me, I thought. Ginger stood out like a sore thumb, even in a crowd. The ball cap and sunglasses were a worthless cover as long as I was with her. My friend's presence was almost like a flashing neon sign shouting out, "Here she is!"

I shrugged. "I'm not sure what you are talking about."

"About Jesus," he said in a hushed tone. "It was him, wasn't it?"

I stood up to leave. "Why are you asking?"

He shook his head, and in a surprisingly sincere tone, he said, "I just need to know, that's all."

Then Ginger spoke up, "You seemed to know it all when you talked to the TV guy."

He nodded. "Well, I was just excited and upset. I got arrested and put in jail. And I know that was my fault. But I had to talk to someone. Everyone thought I was making up a story, just telling a big lie. You gotta admit seeing Jesus is no everyday event."

I glanced at Ginger who gave a bit of a shrug. We both accepted his sincerity.

"You have to believe your own eyes, I guess," I said. "If you thought you saw Jesus, then you might have."

He stared at me and then nodded slowly. "You know, I really did start going to church. And I quit drinking, too."

"That's good," I said. "You're better off, that's for sure."

"I think so," he said, smiling. "Well, I guess I better get along. I just wanted to see you. I've been looking for y'all for weeks now. You don't have to say anything about him. I believe it was him."

And with that, he left. He didn't even ask our names. It seemed clear to me that the man—the paper had said his name was Ballard—was genuine in his repentance. He wanted nothing from me but some hint that what he saw was real.

We stayed at the park for a few minutes more, then got up and began the walk back to the dorm.

Just then I saw a man about thirty yards away holding a camera with a long telephoto lens. I heard the whirring noise of the automatic film advance, pulling through frame after frame.

Someone had set us up! We kept walking, but I smiled wistfully. "We've been hoodwinked by that joker," I said.

"What? You mean—"

"Yeah, he set us up so the photographer would know who to shoot." I put a hand to my head in a gesture of anguish. "How could I have been so dumb? I believed him."

Ginger laughed. "Is it such a big deal? Come on."

Then to my surprise she faced the direction of the photographer, put a hand on her hip, and leaned forward with a phony smile. With her bulging belly, she looked utterly absurd—in a charming way.

"What are you doing?" I cried in baffled surprise.

"It's my Marilyn Monroe look," she cried, still laughing. "Let's give him something to shoot."

"You are flat crazy," I said, grinning. "Let's get back to the dorm."

At that moment, I looked across the street. There was a woman standing there gazing at us. It took my brain a few seconds to register the face. Then it struck me. She was the person standing behind me that day. She was the one who had looked so startled by the events. It must have been her who contacted the photographer, or the news agency that hired him. When she saw me looking at her, she turned away.

"Hope they're paying you some good money," I said, although she probably did not hear the words.

So I was not wrong about that Ballard fellow, the former loud-mouth and drunk. Indeed, he was telling the truth. Well, I thought, some people can change for the better. And maybe I wasn't so dumb after all.

19

In early May we found an apartment that would be available by the end of the term. It had a living room, two bedrooms, and a large kitchen. It wasn't the greatest place in the city, but it would do temporarily. We made a deal with the landlord to take it on a month-to-month basis. That way if we found something better, we could bail out.

In addition, I had a good interview for a job with the newspaper, and expected to be hired. It was part-time in the classified ads section. I would answer the telephone and place customers' advertising requests.

It would not make me rich, but it was something steady and with help from Ginger's parents we could get by.

Amid all the things that were happening, including finals, Ginger and I managed to run out of shampoo and conditioner, and some other things. So one evening we drove out to a Wal-Mart to get the items we needed. As we were checking out, I heard Ginger let out a surprised moan, one that was tinged with excitement.

"Look at that," she said in a hushed tone as she pointed at the rack that was loaded with tabloids and movie-star magazines. On one of the tabloids was a sub-headline that read, "Jesus Visits Alabama College Student."

We grabbed it, paid the bill, and then hurried out. In the car we turned on the dome light and flipped to the inside page for the story. There we were in the picture, the one where Ginger was flashing a pretentious smile and I was looking ahead, my features concealed by the ball cap and sunglasses.

"Nobody can tell who I am," I said with an accusing tone. "But they'll know you, and some of them will put two-and-two together."

Sure enough, at one of my classes the following day, the instructor had a copy of the tabloid, and held it up before we took the exam.

"If some of you pray before taking a test," he said cynically, "you don't have to go far. According to this bulwark of journalistic integrity, Jesus Christ has been present on this very campus." He grinned as his words brought chuckles from some of the students.

I kept my eyes down on my backpack, avoiding the side glances some were making at me.

Finally one girl, who had been eyeing me suspiciously for several moments, leaned over toward my desk and in a stage whisper said, "Was that you at the park?"

It was a good time to fake deafness. "What? What about the park?"

But by then the instructor called the class to order, and began passing out the test sheets. I hurried through the exam, stood up and walked briskly out of the classroom.

When I returned to the dorm that afternoon, I was shocked to see a group of girls in the hallway outside our room. The door was open and Ginger was just inside as though standing guard. It was clear what had happened. Some had recognized her picture in the tabloid and guessed that I was the mystery girl who had been visited by a divine being, namely Jesus Christ.

As I drew nearer, they all turned and began chattering at once.

"What did he say to you?" one of them called, her voice rising above the others.

Then they all gathered around me, babbling in a wild mixture of sounds that resembled an orchestra warming up before a concert.

I waved my hands and got immediate silence.

"Look, I don't know what y'all have heard or seen, but it's nothing that I really want to talk about yet," I said. "I don't feel I'm anyone special. I just don't know why this took place, but it was a private thing. He came for a short visit, then he was gone."

"Was it really him?" one cried.

Then another called, "Is he coming back?"

"Did he say when?"

I shook my head. "He didn't say when he might come back, or where. I'll just have to wait . . . and wonder about it. I'm not trying to hide anything from you, I just don't want it to turn into some kind of circus."

"Hey, don't hide it," one shouted. "This is your chance to be famous. You need to be on Oprah. Really!"

"Really," I repeated crisply, staring at her. "You think that's what this is about? Getting on Oprah?"

"Okay, guys, that's all," Ginger cried, coming to the rescue. "We are not even sure we saw anything. The guy that talked to the TV people was drunk at the time. How reliable is that?"

She meant well, but it didn't satisfy the crowd. More were coming up to the room. I just wanted to get inside and get something to eat, and then rest a little before studying for the other exams.

I turned sideways and managed to slip through the cluster of students, some of whom reached out to touch my arm or shoulder. Then I was in the room. Ginger was in the doorway, blocking any attempts by the others to enter. Then she closed the door.

Letting out a deep breath she uttered, "Wow! Is this going to keep on? You know it made TV again last night."

"It could get worse," I said. "You know, I think it might be time to tell my mom and dad about this. They need to know."

"That's a ten-four, buddy," Ginger said, nodding in approval.

I sat on the edge of the bed, picked up the phone and dialed. Mom answered.

"It's me," I said, my voice sounding just a little weary. "You been watching TV lately?"

"You mean about the divine visitor to UAB?" she said, a hint of laughter in her voice. "We watched the news last night. Your daddy said it almost sounded like you."

I looked up at the ceiling. "Dad said that?"

"Well, of course he was joking," she said. "But I went to the store today and people there were talking about it. One man said the end of the world is near." Then, in a more sober tone, she asked. "Is everything all right there?"

"We're fine, Mom. I just thought I'd call you."

"How about Ginger? She doing okay?"

"Oh, yeah, she's just fine," I said. "We've checked out one apartment that looks good; we're pretty sure we'll take it. And I may have a job lined up."

Then she switched the conversation back. "It sure is strange how people see things. Like that woman from Romania or somewhere who came to Alabama and claimed she saw the Blessed Virgin Mary. I never did believe that. Neither did your daddy."

"Who knows what people see," I remarked dryly.

I glanced over at Ginger who was standing by her bed, watching me. I shrugged and shook my head. She grinned. Then she raised her fist and shook it . . . a signal to plow ahead and tell all.

"Mom," I said, then hesitated. There was a long silence.

"What is it?" she asked.

"I was just going to tell you that Dad's guess was right," I said.

A long, stunned silence followed. "What?"

"It was me. I was the student who the TV people were talking about," I said. It occurred to me that there was a strange feeling of calm over me, now that she had been told.

She didn't say anything, but I heard a distinct gasp. Then, "Abbie, are you joking with me? If you are—"

"No, Mom. I am not joking, believe me," I said. "Somebody's already taken a picture of me. It was in one of the tabloids. I'm sure others are looking for me. And somebody there will see it. They sell those papers at Pop Jackson's store."

Another pause. Then, speaking in a flat monotone, she said, "Well, I just don't know what to think anymore. I just don't know."

She didn't believe me! My own mother was doubting me?

"Mom, I saw what I saw." Then I couldn't think of anything else to say. For a time there was a tense stillness. Then, "Mom, I wasn't the only one. Ginger says she caught a glimpse of him. And the man that was on TV said—"

"He was drunk!" she cut in sharply. "They arrested him, the police did."

I took a deep breath, and tried to calm down. This conversation was starting to get out of control.

"Mom, this is me," I said. "Your daughter. I saw him. It's not like someone seeing a flying saucer. I didn't go to anyone.

It was the police report that got in the newspapers here. And it was the drunk that talked to the news people, not me. And he wasn't that drunk."

She was obviously distressed by the fact that I might be made into a laughingstock. It was something that would reflect on her and my father. It was a thought that concerned me as well.

"Well, we can talk about this when you get home," she said with a note of finality.

"Okay, Mom."

I hung up the phone and looked up at Ginger.

"Sounds like your folks aren't too happy about all this," she said.

"Not too happy at all," I agreed.

Ginger sat down on her bed and stared at me. "You know, your mom is just worried about you. She doesn't want a lot of people bothering her little girl. Mothers are like that."

"I know, but she's also very doubtful about it." Then I shrugged. "Why should this worry me. Jesus is on my side. Who knows, when he comes back, maybe others will see him, and people won't think I'm a kook."

She smiled. "True. Let's just hope he shows back up."

20

Classes ended and Ginger and I packed our things and made the move to our new home, an apartment in a brown-brick structure in Birmingham's Southside area, about four blocks from the campus. In the living room was a fake fireplace with a mantel above. It was the perfect place to put the pink angel.

The job with the paper worked out fine, even though I would have rather been writing news stories. But handling classified ads wasn't too bad. With that modest income, and help from Ginger's parents, we could squeak by month to month. We even had a little money to shop for baby things.

The hot days of June were upon us, and Ginger was in a state of misery whenever she went outside. The heat was oppressive.

Glenn Lyons would call several times a week. He was staying for summer classes, hoping to get his degree at the end of the fall term. I still had not rejoined the Christian group, but told him I might.

One afternoon he called, and I picked up the phone. He asked me again about coming back to the meetings. I promised again to consider it.

"Maybe we should join your group," he told me.

"My group?"

There was a pause. Then with just a hint of humor in his voice, he said, "I saw the picture in that tabloid. Was that Ginger with you?"

"Ginger? What do you mean?"

It occurred to me then that Glenn had never seen Ginger. They had talked on the phone, but never in person.

Then he said, "I saw the picture and it looked like it might have been you. Was it? And was that Ginger with you?"

There was no need to be coy about it. I took a deep breath, then said, "Yeah, Glenn, that was me and that was Ginger."

"I never knew she was pregnant," he said. Then, "She married?"

"No, no she's not," I said. "But we shouldn't be too judgmental, Glenn. There just wasn't a need to bring it up. She could have told you if she wanted."

"I wasn't being judgmental," he said quickly. "Well, I guess she could have told me if she wanted. It's not a subject that would come up in a casual conversation."

Then I laughed. "You know what, Glenn?"

"What?"

"We're talking about Ginger being pregnant," I said, "and not once have you asked me if it was me that 'claimed' to see Jesus. Talk about priorities."

"That's right," he agreed with good humor. "First things first, you know."

"You two do talk a lot," I noted. "I guess maybe you should meet her sometime."

"That would be nice," he said. "When is her baby due?"

"Middle of July, I think," I said. "But babies come when they're ready."

"Getting close to the time," Glenn said. He paused. "Well, I was going to mention the group again. But let me ask you, since you raised the question: Was it you that saw him?"

"Yes it was," I said firmly, and without any mirth. "It was me, Glenn."

There was a long pause. Then, "Well, if it matters to you, I believe you."

"It matters, it really does. Thanks, Glenn." Then I glanced at the alarm clock by the bed. "Guess I have to go now. I have a job, you know. Gotta be on time."

As I was getting ready, I heard the phone ring again. Ginger got it, calling out, "Hey, Glenn. How are you?"

I smiled and shook my head. Sounds like old friends talking, I thought.

Then I went into the heat to drive the green car to work. As I was navigating the streets, my thoughts turned to his next visit. Maybe he would just appear in the old car. After all, he had once done a tune-up on it.

No, he would show up when he was ready, I told myself. But then as I thought about it, it dawned on me that over three months had passed since that day at the park. The flurry of news reports had died down. Maybe the next visit would not spark a lot of coverage.

My job was about what I expected: lots of telephone calls, some from irate people who didn't like a story in the paper that criticized President Bush. I would transfer them to the editorial department. A few times callers wanted to talk about why we were in Iraq.

"Sir, that's not my department," I would say, although it was a question that was very much on my mind. But I never said anything, just transferred them.

On the third evening I was there, one of my co-workers, a young woman with curly blonde hair and a tight skirt, came to my desk. "Say, can I ask you something?" she said.

I nodded. "Sure. Go ahead."

"Well, I don't want to appear nosy or anything," she said, her face flushing slightly, "but are you the girl at UAB that they talked about one night on TV?"

"On TV?" I asked. "What was I supposed to be doing?"

She glanced about, a bit uncomfortable. Then she said, "Well, it was supposedly the girl who claimed she saw . . . you know, Jesus."

I nodded and in a bland voice declared, "Some people think it was me."

She blinked and backed up a few inches. "Oh, I was just wondering. Okay."

Well, I thought, it was an honest answer—some people did think it was me. Correctly.

Then the phone rang, and I thought, "Just in the nick of time." The blonde returned to her own desk.

And then it seemed the interest in the divine visit faded away, and once again all the news was about Iraq and President Bush, the CIA, Karl Rove, Hillary Clinton and the unusual weather activity in the tropics.

For me life seemed a little hum-drum. I liked the job all right, but spending a summer in the city was not suiting me well. It was too hot. I missed being home in Winter Chapel. There was not so much pavement. Grass and trees kept it cooler.

But Ginger made it all worthwhile. Even though her time was drawing near, she kept a great sense of humor and continued to do more than her share around the apartment.

Her parents showed up one July afternoon with a cradle and boxes of baby things. It emphasized the fact that life was going to be a lot different in a short time. I didn't realize how soon it would change.

A few days later I finished my shift and returned to my summer home. It was a sticky July night with droves of flying bugs swarming everywhere. After eating, we heard thunder from over the horizon. I went out on our little porch to watch the flashes of lightning in the distance. A sudden breeze rustled down the street, making the oak trees bend; it chased away the heat and the choking humidity.

The thunder grew louder, closer. I remembered as a child being afraid of thunder. Then I smiled. There was no need for me to be frightened anymore.

That's when I heard Ginger cry out. "Abbie! Abbie! Hurry!"

I dashed inside. She was doubling over on the couch. "Oh my gosh," I cried. "Is this it?"

"Oh, yeah! Please help! I think it's time, I think it's time."

"I'll get the car," I shouted. "Don't worry. Where are the keys, where are the darn keys!"

"Don't know," she moaned. "Just hurry!"

The keys were discovered on top of the refrigerator. Grabbing them I ran outside, then came to a halt. What was I doing? There was no need to get the car. It was out front. She could just go with me. I dashed back inside.

"Come on!" I cried. "Don't be scared. Everything's gonna be okay. Come on, I'll get you out to the car."

I helped her up and we hurried at a fast walk, with me holding her arm as she doubled over in anguish. It was starting to rain as I helped her into the front seat. Then I hurried around to the driver's side, got in, and turned the ignition.

Nothing. Good Lord, I thought. It was dead! The motor made a sick sound as it turned slightly, coughed once, and then went still.

"Oh, great!" I cried. "We've never had a lick of trouble. Now it quits!"

"Lord help me," Ginger muttered.

She was suddenly getting religion, I thought.

"I'll call a cab," I said. "Don't worry."

The rain was falling harder now and the lightning was exploding in the skies above us. And it was scary once again, just as it had been when I was a little girl.

Getting to the porch I thought it would be wasting time looking up the number of a taxi company. I raced into the house, grabbed the phone off the wall and called Glenn.

When he answered, I shouted, "Can you get over here? My car won't start and Ginger's in labor!"

"What? Right now?"

"Yes, yes, right now! Can you get over here?"

"I'm on my way!"

I double-timed to the car and leaned outside the passenger side. "Glenn's coming over."

Grimacing, Ginger uttered, "Glenn! Why didn't you call nine-one-one?"

I slapped my forehead. I didn't even think of 911. "It was quicker to call Glenn," I said. "What does it matter who we call? You just gotta get to the hospital!"

A few minutes later Glenn came tearing down the street like he was in the Talladega 500. The car squealed to a stop and he jumped out.

"Y'all ready?" he cried, the words laced with panic.

I helped Ginger from my car, got her into Glenn's, and then hastily started for the apartment.

"Let me lock the door before we go!" I called.

Apparently all Glenn heard was the word "go." And he floored it.

"Hey! Hold up!" I screamed. But to no avail. I wondered why I was so intent on locking the door anyway. I just wasn't thinking right. I watched the taillights grow more distant and heard the tires whine at the intersection.

Standing there getting soaked, with lightning bolts flashing around me, I threw a salute to the night and muttered, "Nice going, Glenn."

Then I paused, letting the rain take a good shot at me. I was dripping wet. Maybe now was a good time for him to show back up. I looked up at the sky, the rain splattering my face. More thunder rumbled, but that was it. Nobody appeared.

My shoes squished as I walked slowly to the apartment. There was no great need for haste now. Warm, dry clothing was in order, as was a change of shoes. Then the reality struck me that I couldn't go to the hospital anyway, because the car wouldn't start. After all these months running like a top, why did it choose tonight to quit on me?

I called the emergency room to see if they got there in one piece. A nurse confirmed that they had arrived but said she couldn't tell me anything further. Then I called Ginger's folks and told them they were about to become grandparents. Mr. Burns thanked me for the call and said they would be coming in the morning. It was polite and cool.

Then I called my mother. She was ecstatic, ready to come to Birmingham right then.

"Mom, let's wait until her parents get here," I said. "Besides who can say this is the real thing. It could be hours. I mean, I've heard horror stories about women being in labor for thirty-six to forty hours."

"I know all about that," she reminded me. "I was in labor with your brother for nearly a day. But sometimes people don't even make it to the hospital."

The mention of Austin brought a moment of silence. I could almost see the expression on her face. Then I said, "Well, it's better to wait. Besides, it's storming. Not a good night to be driving."

"Well, we'll come see the baby once Ginger is home."

We said good-bye then, and I walked out onto the porch. The thunder and lightning had moved on, but a soft rain still fell. Should I call the hospital again? For all the running around I did, and the phone calls, I still managed to have the keys in my hand. I went back to the car to give it another try.

To my amazement, the old Cutlass cranked right up. I left it running while I ran back and locked the apartment door. Then I drove to the hospital.

In the waiting room Glenn was standing by the window, watching the drizzle that put jelly-like beads on the glass.

I tapped him on the shoulder. "Anything yet?"

"No. Not yet. She's in the delivery part though."

"Thanks for leaving me in the rain," I said, grinning.

"What? I thought you said for me to go," he said. "And that's what I did."

I laughed. "Well, it's okay. I got my car started. I mean it just started up, not that I had anything to do with it."

He gazed at me with a vacant expression. "Your car started? That's good."

So we waited, drinking coffee and talking about the challenges of caring for a baby.

I closed my eyes for a time, and almost drifted off, when vaguely I became aware of a nurse calling for Burns. "Anyone with the Burns family?"

"Here," I said. "We're here."

She announced in a happy voice, "It's a little girl." Then, looking at Glenn, she said, "Are you the daddy?"

Glenn's face turned scarlet. "No . . . I mean—a girl? Is she okay?"

"A girl!" I called in a delayed reaction. "That's great."

"Everybody's fine," the nurse said, still puzzled that Glenn was not the father. "You can see her in a little while. We got some things to do. Then you can also see the baby."

A little later I went in to see Ginger. She was exhausted, but had a happy glow about her.

"Hey, roomie," she said, reaching out a hand to me. "The tough part is over."

"I called your folks," I told her. "They said they'd be up tomorrow sometime. You came through like a trouper."

"Good. Is Glenn still here?"

"Yeah, he's out there," I said. "The nurse thought he was the father."

"Oh, no. Poor Glenn." Ginger managed a laugh. "Did he say he was innocent?"

"He looked stunned," I gushed. "You should have seen the look. I thought he would collapse."

She laughed again. Then I went back to the waiting room, and Glenn went in to see her. It occurred to me that they had finally met face-to-face in that wild ride.

Looking out the window I saw the clouds breaking up, revealing a slice of moon that rode through the dark sky. The rain had tapered off, and only a few large silvery spikes of water streamed down from the roof. A new life, I thought, staring at the dripping rain water. My brother is killed and is out of our world, but someone new comes in to touch my life.

21

Ginger brought her baby home several days later, and for a time things were hectic at our little apartment. Her parents came up as promised, and the day after that Mom and Dad showed up.

At first, Dad could not hide his displeasure with a baby coming out of wedlock. He complained that he had been kept in the dark. But Mom toned him down, saying, "If we told you it would have made you mad as a hornet. Look at you now."

Finally he eased up, even allowing himself to praise the beauty of the baby.

He brightened up even more when he heard that Ginger had named her Madeline Abigail.

When Ginger told me of the name, I don't think I had ever been more flattered.

Of course, Glenn came by several times. It was obvious to me that he had more than a Good Samaritan's interest in Ginger.

And so that episode of our lives was over. The baby had been a center of attention since the fall of 2004. Now that she was safely here, it was time for all of us to move ahead with our lives.

The summer passed swiftly and suddenly it was time to start classes again. Ginger had decided to sit out the term, which would allow her time to take care of Ms. Madeline Abigail Burns. But at the same time her parents had asked her to come home to Howton Crossroads, so they could help her with the baby. I had a feeling that Ginger might take them up on the offer.

Ginger was torn by the situation, wanting to stay with me and stick to our agreement to grind our way through this part of our lives, working, going to school, and taking care of the infant. But it was a pretty big order for two girls who had never had to take care of a baby before. Her mother could and would provide top-grade expertise in child rearing.

I knew that and so did Ginger.

"What do you think?" she asked me.

"Well, Ginger, it's really a no-brainer," I said. "You were worried your folks would want nothing to do with the baby. Now they are begging to help. You have to let them."

"You won't be mad at me?" she asked, holding her hands up to her chin, almost in prayer.

"Mad? Of course not. I mean, we'll be able to visit and talk," I said. "And we'll always be best friends. Nothing can change that."

She threw her arms around me. "Abbie, you are the best friend anyone could ever have."

I returned the hug and muttered, "Times two, roomie. Times two."

And so the day we knew was coming arrived in August 2005. We talked about it over breakfast, when the baby was asleep.

"In the back of my mind I figured this might happen," I said. "It's probably for the best. Your Mom will help you with the baby a lot more than I can."

Blinking back tears, Ginger forced a smile. "It's not going to be the same without you, Abbie."

"Aw, go on," I blurted. "You'll be fine. But I will miss that baby."

"Yeah, you don't need an alarm clock with her around."

I stirred the bowl of cereal, trying to think of what to say. Bidding good-bye to a friend was a new and scary thing . . .

it reminded me of the time when Austin left. We hadn't said much. He just left.

Looking up from the cereal, I saw Ginger was biting her lip.

"How long have we known each other?" she asked.

"Right at twelve months," I said.

"That's enough time to be best friends forever," she said. "Seems like we've known each other all our lives."

"We'll always be best friends," I promised.

Then she made a great effort to laugh. "Who else could get me a chance to see Jesus Christ in person?"

Nodding, I replied, "I wanted to show you a spectacular time that day."

"You did that, all right," she said. Then she grabbed some napkins and wiped her eyes. "I'll never forget it. You gonna call me if he comes back?"

"Count on it," I said. "And there is no 'if' to it. He's coming back."

She and the baby left Friday, a day the radio news was talking about a hurricane named Katrina that was entering the Gulf of Mexico.

I packed up my things and moved back into the dorm. This was my sophomore year. To be sure, I had barely passed the first year, because of the time off I had taken after my brother's death. It had been catch-up most of the way. I planned to do better.

But college didn't seem the same anymore. I missed Ginger. My new roommate was a girl from Georgia named Carla Whitfield, a petite brunette who wanted to be a gymnast. Although we were courteous to one another, we never became friends. She went her way, I went mine. In fact, at times she appeared to be avoiding me. That can be an awkward way to exist.

I wondered about her cool manner. One day one of the girls

on the floor told me that Carla had made some remarks about me, that she was uneasy being around "a Jesus freak."

But then, she wasn't the only one. My own mother still had some grave misgivings.

In fact, she and Dad had taken it upon themselves to get me an appointment with a psychologist. At first I refused, but she and Dad came to Birmingham the day of the appointment and insisted that it would help for me to talk to him.

22

H is name was Alvin Glucksman and his office was only a few blocks from the campus. He was a husky man with brown hair and dark eyes that sparkled. He had high cheek bones and appeared to be amused.

He met me at the door of his office and gestured to a maroon easy chair. Then he pulled a smaller chair closer and sat down, a yellow note pad on his lap.

"So tell me what's been going on with you," he said. "Abbie is it? You prefer that to Abigail?"

I laughed. "Yes, Abbie is fine."

"All right, Abbie it is. So tell me about these visits."

I shrugged. "There's not much to tell. I just saw this man who . . . who was Jesus. He didn't have to tell me who he was."

"Uh-huh. And you saw him how many times?"

"Two . . . two so far," I said hesitantly. Strange how my confidence seemed to erode when questioned about it.

"So far?" He nodded, raised his eyebrows, and scribbled some notes. "He said he would be coming back?"

"Yes, sir, he said he would."

"I see." He wrote a few more lines. Then he looked at me again. "Now when you saw him, were you alone or—well, were there others around? Other people?"

"The first time I was alone," I said. "The second time there were a lot of people. I guess maybe two hundred or so. And several also saw him. Three for sure saw him."

He put the note pad aside and stared at me. "Okay, that was the time at the park on campus, right?"

I nodded. "Right. That got into the paper and on TV news and all that."

Dr. Glucksman jotted more notes. Then, putting the pad aside again, he asked, "You sleep all right, Abbie? I mean in recent months. Since these visions started?"

"Sleep?" I paused to think. "Yeah, I guess. I didn't for a time there, just after my brother was killed. I didn't sleep well at all then."

"Yes, I read that about your brother," he said, scanning the questionnaire I had filled out. "I'm so sorry. That must have bothered you a lot."

"It did. A lot." I raised a hand to halt the questions for a moment. "I wanted to say something if I can."

"Sure. Go right ahead."

"When I saw him at the park and it got on the news and all, I didn't call them," I explained. "I didn't call reporters or anything. Somebody else did that. I wasn't looking for publicity or anything like that."

He nodded. "All right. Now, you were saying you didn't sleep well after your brother was killed. Did it bother you in other ways?"

"It did," I said.

"How? In what ways?"

"It made me angry at my religion," I said, nodding. "Quit going to church at that time. And threw away a statue of an angel that had been in the family for years and years. I guess I just rebelled in general. I stayed out of school for about three weeks or so, sort of fell behind."

He didn't say anything, but made notes, a frown causing creases to form like waves across his forehead. Then, finished with writing, he glanced at me and smiled.

"You and your brother were close?" he asked.

"Yes, sir. We grew up together. We were the only children."

"I see. It must have been rough on you." Then he pointed the pad at me. "How do you feel . . . how do you feel about the war?"

"How do I feel?" I shrugged. "I don't know. At first I thought it was the right thing. But now I hate it because it killed my brother. I feel that in a way we should not even be there where so many guys have been killed or maimed, not to mention the civilians, especially the Iraqi children. I just think it was a mistake to be there."

"Did you feel that way before your brother was killed?"

"There was always concern about it," I said. "There was always worry about him."

"Um-hmm."

"Oh, and one other thing," I volunteered. "In addition to a worry about Iraq, my roommate, my best friend, was pregnant at the time. I was worried about her. That is the point I want to make."

I waited while he wrote some more. Then, in a low voice, he asked, "Are you sleeping better now?"

"Yes. A little better, I guess." I frowned at his interest in sleep.

He leaned over and tossed the pad onto his desk. "You know, Abbie, sometimes stress and worry can do a lot of things to our minds and bodies that we're not always aware of."

I stared at him. Then, I said, "You mean like seeing things that aren't there?"

"Well, no, I didn't mean that you didn't see somebody," he explained. "But you did have a lot on your mind."

"It wasn't that much," I countered.

He raised a hand and began counting off on the fingers: "Your brother is killed; there's the anger over religion; you're worried about your pregnant friend; you're falling behind in your studies. Just one of these would have an impact on the strongest individual. Put them all together, and that's a formula for the brain to rebel."

I turned my eyes from him and focused on a tree that was framed in the window. "Well, all that does not explain why somebody else saw him, too."

He nodded. "No, it does not. But let's just stick to what you say you saw, not what somebody else might have seen."

I said little more after that, and concluded that this visit was a waste of time. If I was having mental problems, then they would either clear up or get worse. Either way, I was certain of what I had seen and heard.

We left then and Mom and Dad took me to dinner. We ate in awkward silence. When there was talk, it was stilted and had a phony edge to it. They asked very little about the session. Dad suggested that at the end of the sophomore year I might try for a summer job with one of the TV stations.

"That sounds like a wonderful idea," Mom added, as though she were reading from a script.

"It might work out," I said, my words listless.

"It's the right path if you want to be a TV anchor one day," Dad said, chewing on a toothpick and regarding me closely.

The talk was off the mark. It was just jostling around, while they really wondered what the psychologist said. So I put the subject on the table.

"The doctor doesn't think I'm ready for the mental ward yet," I flatly declared.

"Abbie," Mom said softly. "Don't talk like that. We know

you're all right. It's just—you've had a lot on your mind."

"That's exactly what he said," I agreed. "But I didn't make anything up. And I didn't call the press."

Dad put his hands up in a gesture of peace. "Let's just all talk about it later on. Maybe when you get home for Christmas." Then, as if to make amends, he said, "Say, Abbie. I've been looking at a nice, fairly new Ford. You need something better and you just might like this one."

I gave him one of those "nice try" looks, and then said, "The Cutlass is doing okay, Dad. Thanks."

They hugged me, and then drove back to Winter Chapel. I went back to my room. Carla was there, but we did not speak. I read for a while before falling asleep.

The next morning I awoke, aware of a dream I had about Ginger and Austin coaxing me to go on an airplane ride with them, although neither could fly. The flight was to be across a lake. I couldn't remember the rest.

It was a strange dream. Maybe I was going crazy, I thought.

23

One bright October afternoon I returned to the dorm to find a message for me. Ginger had called. The message was simple. "Call me."

I dialed the number. Mrs. Burns answered. She sounded full of cheer. "Abbie!" she exclaimed. "How are you? You should see the baby. Growing like all get-out. I'll get Ginger."

I heard the baby crying in the background.

"Hey, roomie, what's happening?" Ginger's voice was filled with vim and vigor.

"Great," I said. "You sound all happy and content. You must be eating good."

"Yeah boy!" she said. "Me and Mom are getting to know one another again. It's great Abbie. And I hope Madeline Abigail grows up to be just like you."

"Well, maybe," I said. "Maybe not."

"Hey, is something wrong?" she said. "Tell me, has your friend showed back up? I've been wondering about it."

"No, no he hasn't. Not yet."

"But he will," she said in an uplifting tone. "I know he will, Abbie. Have a little faith. Did I tell you? I've started going to church with Mom and Dad."

I grinned. "That's good, Ginger. Proud of you. It's good if that's what you decide. Like I always said, it's your call."

There was a pause. Then she asked, "What about you?"

"Not yet," I said. "I sit at the dorm sometimes and look at

the pink angel. That's my church for now. Did I tell you I had to see a psychologist? It was my parents' idea. They insisted."

"That was crazy," she said. "You saw what you saw. And I saw him, too." Then, changing the subject, she said, "Hey, why don't you come down here for Thanksgiving? Spend a few days with me. Then I'll bring Madeline Abigail and visit your home around Christmas time. Is that okay with you? Ask your folks."

It was overwhelming. "That sounds like an awesome idea," I cried. "There's no need to ask my folks. You are always welcome without calling. Just show up. Mom will flip to see that baby."

So it was settled. Our holiday plans were firmed up. The days seemed to sparkle knowing that my best friend would be back in my life. I thought how much brighter Christmas would be, in contrast with the bleak Christmas of 2004 and my brother's death.

That evening I sat on my bed and pondered. When was my special visitor coming back? Months had passed since that day at the park. He had said he would come again. But there had been so many questions about it. And my parents' doubts about what and who I had seen.

The days of autumn passed over the state in gold and red hues, like honey and wine spilling over the land. I was doing fine in my studies, and looking to the future. I had everything to look forward to.

My mother was a little upset when I told her of spending Thanksgiving with Ginger's family, but rebounded happily when she was told Ginger and the baby would be at our house for a few days at Christmas.

THANKSGIVING AT GINGER'S was a lot like it was at our home. Some of the children who lived down the road came up before dinner and we took time to play tag with them. Then we stuffed ourselves with ham and turkey and her mother's homemade sweet potato pie.

Afterwards, Ginger and I spent hours talking and laughing about our year in college together. Then, in the evening after a light snack, she stood up and said, "Here, I got something you might like."

She returned with a CD. "Listen to this. I got it so it would remind me of you and your brother. Because, in a way, it was like I knew him."

It was the sound track from the movie, *The Last of the Mohicans.*

I listened without a word. But I nodded in appreciation.

After a few minutes, I said, "Thanks, roomie. He would have liked it that you thought highly of Hawkeye." She laughed and nodded. I continued, "Now, we look forward to Christmas. You come up. And bring that baby, you hear?"

"Oh, yes, I hear," she said. "And is it okay if I bring a friend?"

I looked at her quizzically. "A friend? Who?"

"Oh, some guy I met." She grinned, baiting me to ask about him. "I really like him."

I shrugged. "Well, of course. Bring him along. We'll find a place for him."

The next morning early we said good-bye. Ginger had happy tears and hugged me. "Can't wait to see you at Christmas in Winter Chapel."

"Times two," I said. Then I left for the drive back.

24

I was hitting the books hard and doing my best to make good grades in all my classes, because school work was the main thing in my life . . . except in the back of my mind there was the constant question of when Jesus would return.

I went to the park several times, but there was no sign of him.

One of the days it was cool and sunny, and I sat on a bench waiting, my chin down in my jacket, trying to keep warm. I stayed there for about two hours until a couple of panhandlers came by and started making remarks that were improper, to say the least. Another time it was drizzling, and I was the only one there. That time I stayed only a few minutes.

But the autumn days were passing and winter was near at hand. Finals were coming up and then it would be the Christmas break. Despite the exams, there was an overwhelming need to go home, tests or no tests. So that weekend, I got into the green car and headed east toward home.

On the drive, I looked up and saw a flight of wild geese passing overhead in the usual V formation. It made me stop the car and get out for a better view. It was a majestic sight.

It was something Austin and I would do even when we were teenagers—sit on the hill and look up in an autumn sky and watch for such a flight. Only once did we see it, but it left us with a great feeling of awe, a sense that all was well in the universe.

That same feeling passed over me now as I watched. It was made more so when my hair was rustled by a sudden breeze.

I arrived late Friday evening, had supper with my parents, then sat in the living room with them talking and drinking hot chocolate. Nothing was said about imagining divine beings or psychologists. We just talked about Christmas and Ginger's visit.

Mom gave a cheerless smile. "I don't know how your dad and I will take to a baby in the house. It's been a long time."

"Old vets like you?" I joshed. "You guys will take it in stride."

She shook her head and gave a slight shrug. She just hadn't got the Christmas spirit yet, I thought.

On Saturday morning I got up and found Mom in the kitchen with toast and fresh coffee waiting for me. We sat at the table.

"Well, anything special you want to do today?" she asked.

"No . . . yes, yes, on second thought," I said. "Mom let's go to the cemetery. I want to go to Austin's grave. I never have gone there. I guess I just wasn't ready. I am now. That's one of the things I feel I want to do. And need to."

"Did the psychologist tell you that?" she asked. "That you needed to go to the grave and visit your brother?"

I grinned at her. "Did you think he should tell me that?"

"Well—I," she stammered. "I don't know. Did he?"

"No, I just want to do it. Nobody has to tell me that." Then I took her hand in mine, and said, "I thought of it all by myself, Mom."

Actually, there were two reasons I wanted to go. First, just to be there, close to where he was. And secondly, I thought there might be a chance it would be the place where Jesus would show back up. If he did so in front of my mother, what more proof would she need?

Then I immediately felt ashamed of myself. I didn't need anyone else to see him. I had seen him and that was enough. There was no need to prove anything, no need at all.

I pulled several of Mom's marigolds from the side of the house. Then we drove her car to the cemetery which was about a mile from the house. I could have walked there, but Mom might have had trouble at that distance.

We pulled up the blacktop driveway and curved around to the site of Austin's grave. It was about fifty feet from the driveway, lying near a huge oak tree that must have been two hundred years old or more. A smaller honey locust was nearer and it hummed as a soft breeze blew over the grounds, tugging at my hair.

I walked ahead of Mom to the grave and placed the flowers on the base of the stone. Grass had grown to cover the rise in the ground. It had turned from green to amber.

"Hello, brother," I whispered. "It's a beautiful day. We miss you. Hope you are well. Wish you could be with us. I love you."

Then Mom came by and put her hand on my elbow. Then she started tearing up.

I turned to her and smiled. "It's okay, Mom. But if you start, I will too. He's okay, I'm sure."

She nodded. "I know. I just wish we could have seen him onc last time."

With that she burst into tears, and then I did, too. I put an arm around her. "Mom, he wouldn't want us to cry."

We stayed for about fifteen minutes, and then turned to go back to the house. Before leaving I went back, and touching the headstone, said, "I will see you soon, brother. Soon."

I was confident of that. I really was.

On the way home we stopped at Jackson's General Store for a few things Mom needed, and I wanted a Coke.

As we were gathering things, Pop, a big, balding man in his late fifties, saw me and called, "Hey, Abbie, do you know the girl they say saw Jesus?"

I glanced at Mom. Her face turned pale and she gave me a horrified look that almost made me burst out in laughter.

"Do I know her?" I repeated, stalling to find the right answer. "Well, yeah, I know who she is. Yes, sir."

By then other patrons had stopped to gawk at me.

And old Aaron Jefferson put in, "Is that the one they talked about on TV?"

"Yeah," said Pop. "It was all the news for a while there."

Then I volunteered, "I think it's kind of died down. She sort of stayed out of sight."

"Can't blame her," Aaron opined. "Who wants all those liberal news people down here?"

"Well, I don't know about that," Pop countered. "We was just saying back then that wouldn't it be something if it turned out to be Abbie Staley." Then he laughed again. "It sure would put Winter Chapel on the map."

"It sure would, Pop," I said solemnly.

Then I turned away and walked to the cooler to find a drink. Mom told me to hurry, that we had things to do. Then she began explaining to Pop that she planned to wax the kitchen floor and maybe do some painting before the next rain came. She kept talking the whole time we checked out, keeping anyone else from breaking in with any comment on the girl who claimed to have seen Jesus.

I just smiled and said nothing.

Sunday evening, I returned to Birmingham to prepare for the exams. After an hour or so, I put the books aside and went to sleep. The next few days I ripped through the tests, wound up my housekeeping chores at the dorm room, and then packed stuff up and prepared to return home. It would have to be a better Christmas in 2005 than the one the year before. Before leaving I made a special effort to be a good person and awoke Carla.

She aroused and looked up at me with surprise and a trace of disgust.

"Hey. Just wanted to wish you a merry Christmas," I said.

She turned over and sat up. "Well, thanks. The same to you."

I picked up my suitcase and headed for the door, thinking that some people were just born cantankerous. Then to my surprise I heard her say:

"Wait a minute. Wait, Abbie."

I turned and fixed a curious gaze on her. Thinking, what now?

"I know we haven't been real close or anything," she said. "But that's been my fault. I had heard all that stuff about Jesus and all."

I looked her in the eye. "Yeah? You heard about that, huh?"

"Yes I did. And whatever people want to say doesn't matter. I still think you're okay."

I smiled. "That sounds okay by me. After all we share the same room. Merry Christmas, Carla."

Then I headed for home.

25

An hour and a half later, I was turning from U.S. 78 onto the county road leading to Winter Chapel. I could see it in the distance, the church steeples rising into the blue sky, and the houses gleaming in the sunlight. Some were set on hillsides where they had an almost artistic backdrop of red barns and regal oaks, the gray trees standing proud despite their barren branches.

At the intersection I turned left, noting the beehive of activity at Pop Jackson's store. A mile down the road I came to the driveway and turned in. Mom had put a green wreath on the front door, and smaller ones in the windows.

Coming into the kitchen I found her sitting at the table, looking at a magazine. The stove was cold and there was no aroma of things being baked.

"Hey, your wayward daughter is home," I said. "The merriest to one and all."

She didn't think it was very funny. "Well, how was the tests?"

"I did okay." Then, in a tone of mock anger I said, "Why isn't there some action in this kitchen, Mom? We got company coming."

She looked surprised. "Company? Who?"

"Well, Ginger and the baby are coming. I told you on the phone."

"It just doesn't seem much like Christmas," she said soberly. "I was thinking about the last one. I can't get over it. And I never will."

What could I say? She was right in a way. Yet . . .

"But Mom, if Austin were here he'd tell us to celebrate like always," I protested mildly. "He would want that. And besides, we still have some guests coming. Come on, I'll help you. It's time we spent a few hours together in the kitchen."

After putting my things in the room, I hurried back downstairs. Mom had gotten up and was rumbling around in the cabinet. I asked her for directions on what to do. And so it went, as we began baking for the holiday. Within minutes I was up to my elbows in flour, sugar, and spices. I did not expect it to really take hours, but it did.

By nightfall, we had three cherry pies and four large loaves of bread baked, plus a ham cooked and a turkey ready for the oven. The next day would be the twenty-first, and Ginger would be arriving.

As we cleaned up the mess, I brought up a subject that I knew would upset her.

"Mom, Ginger is bringing a friend with her."

"Oh, who?"

"Well, I don't know. She just said it was a guy she likes. Anyway, he'll probably stay over and I thought he could stay in Austin's room."

She was aghast. Then, in an angry voice, she said, "No, ma'am. I'm not having a stranger using my son's room."

"Okay, okay. Don't get upset." I thought for a moment, then said, "What if me and Ginger sleep in Austin's room and give my room to him."

She shrugged. "Well, that might be all right. He wouldn't care about you being in there."

So that was settled. I slept well that night.

On the next day just before noon, Ginger arrived, shouting out Christmas greetings even before she was in the house. I met her on the porch.

"Oh, that baby is growing," I cried happily. Then I hugged Ginger. "Merry Christmas, roomie."

Then I saw her boyfriend coming up behind her, lugging a suitcase. I was agog.

"Glenn! Glenn! It's you. You're the one?"

He grinned. "Yep, it's me. You okay, Abbie?"

Ginger cried out, "You bet he's the one." Then she laughed. "I wanted to surprise you. I guess I did, didn't I?"

By now Mom had come to the door as we began edging inside.

"Mom, look at that baby," I bragged. "And this is Glenn, the one I had told you about. You remember. He's Ginger's . . . uh, he's her friend. He's the one that drove her to the hospital."

"Oh, yes, I remember," Mom said. She was laughing now as she took the baby from Ginger.

"Let's get inside," I urged. "It's chilly out here."

Once in the living room, Ginger threw out both hands and cried, "So this is Winter Chapel, the place I've heard so much about."

"This is it. This is home, Ginger."

We planned to have the big Christmas dinner that evening, while she was there, and not worry about stuffing ourselves too much on Christmas Eve itself. On Christmas Day Mom and Dad were going to church, and then the three of us were going to the cemetery.

"Come on everybody," Mom said. "Let's go to the kitchen and have a sandwich and some cherry pie. We've got eggnog to drink, or there's tea and coffee."

Ginger was pulling Glenn. "Come on, you can at least have a bite to eat."

He grinned. "Well, I can't stay long. I'll have some coffee and that cherry pie sounds good."

"You're not going to stay?" Mom inquired. "We've got Austin's room open for you."

Mom's willingness to have Glenn stay in Austin's room surprised me. But he insisted he had to leave. He said he would come back on the morning of Christmas Eve to get Ginger and take her home.

Later, after he had gone, I poked her on the arm. "So you two are hitting it off, huh?"

She laughed. "Yeah. He's a great guy, Abbie." Then, in a hushed voice, she confided, "He keeps hinting about wanting to ask me something. I am hoping it involves a ring. Madeline would have a father. No, she would have a dad. You know, like the saying goes, 'Anyone can be a father, but it takes someone special to be a dad.'"

"Wow, it's turning out to be a great Christmas already. You think he's about to ask you?"

She giggled. "You know Glenn. He may need a push from someone."

I slapped her on the shoulder and we both laughed.

That evening we consumed a great feast. Ginger's nonstop commentary kept everyone alert as we enjoyed the festive meal. Her mother was selling the flower shop so she could be home to help raise the baby.

We had coffee in the living room. "Your folks have done a complete turnaround from what you expected," I said.

"I know," she said brightly, a smile lighting up her face. "It just blows me away. They are totally crazy about Madeline Abigail. Totally crazy."

Mom had the baby and clung to her while we sipped coffee and chatted. Then Ginger took her and put her to bed. She and the baby would take Austin's room.

Then we stayed up late talking.

"I want to see your brother's grave tomorrow," she said.

"That's good," I said.

"I saw the football pictures and the CD player up there. It feels almost like he's here."

"Yeah, it does feel like it. We have the medals and stuff the Army sent. We want to put them on the wall, probably in a glassed-in box of some sort. The blue thing is the Combat Infantryman Badge. I never knew about that until he told me once."

Then Ginger asked, "Still no visit?"

"Still no visit," I repeated.

She viewed my answer as being a little negative. "Well, you have to have faith, you know. We've got years and years ahead of us—I hope."

"Ginger," I said slowly, vexed by her view on things, "I don't think he meant years and years."

26

Next morning we put on our jackets and blue jeans and drove over to the cemetery. It was a cold day with the sun breaking through a thickening cover of blue-gray clouds. For a long time we stood by Austin's grave. Ginger bowed her head and said a prayer. When she finished she reached over and squeezed my shoulder.

I glanced over the graveyard which contained some headstones that dated back nearly a hundred and fifty years. "Lots of people here, Ginger."

She put a hand over her eyes to shade them from the sun. "Yep, lots of people."

"Not many of them died fighting for their country like Austin," I said. "Or at least thinking they were defending the country."

She nodded, staring at me. "You think he died for nothing?"

"That's what I think," I said. "He wanted so much to defend us from terrorists, to stop another nine-eleven from happening. But I don't think Iraq was the right place to do that. I believe he was thinking that, too, toward the end."

Ginger nodded. "I never paid much attention for awhile there. But lately I have thought about it, about all those people being killed." She shuddered for a moment.

"It was a mistake going there," I said.

We stood for a while longer, and then she turned to me. "You think we should get back? Your folks are going to be worn out watching my child."

I nodded. "Yeah. We should." Then waving, I said, "See you later, brother."

And Ginger added, "Bye now, Austin."

Back at the house we added a few more Christmas decorations to the tree. Then we sat in the living room and talked. Shortly after noon, the baby fell asleep. After settling her in, Ginger came back downstairs.

She stood before me. "Come on, show me that hill you guys always climbed."

"Well, I—" I shrugged and shook my head. "I don't go up there anymore."

"Why not?" She held a hand out for me to get up. "Come on, it's chilly and gray outside. It's the perfect winter day."

Finally I agreed. "But I don't want to stay long."

We put on coats and toboggan caps, and went out the back door. The day had become grayer, and the air felt sharply cold.

As we walked up the rise, I explained, "You see, after Austin was killed, I said I wouldn't come back up here."

"I understand," Ginger said, looking serious for a change. "But you have to come here sometime, girl. You can't—I don't know, you just can't keep away from something that's been special in your life."

I thought about it a second. Then I nodded. "Maybe you're right, Ginger."

We reached the top just as the sun broke through a bank of clouds. I gazed down on the house and the garden.

"What a view," she said. "You must have really loved this place."

"Oh, naturally, we did."

Then she pointed to the cherry trees. "You told me about those. What's down there?"

"That's the soybean field," I said. "It's sort of overgrown because nobody rented it from Dad. It just sat idle this year."

As we were looking, I noticed a man standing near the edge of the field, by the highway.

"Who's that?" Ginger asked.

I shook my head. "Somebody is always looking at the field, thinking about renting it."

Just then Mom called. "Ginger, the baby's up. You want me to get her?"

"So soon?" she cried in mock anguish. "I better get down there." And away she ran, making a noise like a fire siren on a rescue run.

I laughed and watched as she hurried down the hillside. That girl was crazy. Crazy in a good way. Before leaving, I took a look over at the trees. They were dark and gnarled, the branches intertwined. They needed pruning, I thought.

Just then a sudden breeze rose and sent dead leaves and twigs whirling into the chill air. It tugged at my coat collar, ruffled my hair and caused the bare branches of the cherry trees to make a rasping sound. It grew stronger and turned the air even colder.

And then as quickly as it had started, it died away. There was absolute calm.

Then, from the trees I saw a light, a bright goldish-white, oval-shaped illumination that appeared among the tree branches. And suddenly I saw him standing there, smiling at me. He was here!

This time he was wearing a white robe with a golden cross on the chest. He wore sandals.

"You're here!" I shouted in a cry of pure joy. "You came back!"

I started to run to him but he held a hand up and walked toward me.

"Abbie," he said softly. "I told you I would be back."

Words wouldn't come then and I just stared at him. Where was Ginger? Had she already entered the house? From a distance I heard a man shout followed by the sound of a car horn.

Then he said, "There is someone who wants to see you."

He stepped sideways and there before me was my brother. He was in blue jeans and a green sweater. There was a light golden haze surrounding him, almost a giant halo. He smiled at me the way he always had. There were no signs of wounds, no disfigurement.

I ran to him and threw my arms around him. Was he a spirit that I couldn't touch? No, I could feel his arms and chest as my head rested on him. And I wept.

"Austin! Oh, Austin, I'm so sorry."

"Abbie, it's all right, it's all right," he said, the voice thin. "I'm fine. The worries are over. Don't cry."

"I just can't believe it," I cried. "You're here."

"Abbie, I can't stay long," he said. His voice had an echo-like quality. "I'm here for just a short time. Then I go back. It's only long enough for us to see one another. Take care of Mom and Dad and yourself. And all is well. All is well."

"I miss you, and I love you," I said.

He smiled at me. "Times two."

And then he was gone. For a moment the halo-like form floated before me; then it vanished.

I turned and reached out to touch Jesus. He took my hand. "I will leave now, Abbie. One day, far ahead, I will return. You will see me then. Help one another. Be friends in the spirit."

There were many things I wanted to ask. But all I could do was cry and smile at the same time and hold onto his hand.

"Thank you," I sobbed.

Then he touched my face. His hands were soft and warm. I closed my eyes and felt a great peace come over me. I opened my eyes and looked into his.

"I will miss you very much," I sobbed.

He was walking away. Then he turned and smiled. "Times two," he said.

And then he was gone.

I felt as though my soul was lifted into the heavens in that moment, but my body was absolutely without strength. And I sat down on the hill, and let my head fall almost to my lap.

Be friends in the spirit?

27

S omeone was shaking me, and I heard Ginger's voice calling, "Abbie! Abbie! Are you okay? What happened?"

"What?"

"You okay?"

I blinked several times to clear the cobwebs from my head and eyes. Then, I replied, "Yes, I'm fine." Then I tugged at her jeans. "Ginger, he was here. Just after you left."

She sank down beside me and looked closely into my eyes.

"He was here? And I missed him?"

I shook my head. "I feel funny. Weak. But I saw him and he brought Austin with him."

"Austin?"

She was staring at me like I was mentally unstable. I looked at the brown grass around me. I didn't remember sitting down.

"Abbie, are you okay?"

"I'm fine," I said, glancing at her. "Where's the baby?"

"Your mom has her. We got worried when you didn't come down. You were just sitting here and didn't answer when we called."

"Really? I didn't hear anyone calling. I must have almost fainted, I guess."

Ginger rose and put a hand on my left arm. "Come on up. Can you stand?"

"Sure." I stood up. Granted, I was a little shaky, but otherwise fine. "How about that?" Ginger nodded and smiled. I asked, "And you didn't see him?"

She shook her head. "No. But that's okay, the main thing is that you did."

Now I put a hand on her shoulder. "Wait a minute. You're not putting me on, are you? Do you believe me?"

She nodded. "Yes, you know I do."

Well, I knew a snow job when I saw one. She was patronizing me. She didn't believe it and neither would anyone else. I kept my hand on her shoulder. "Wait. Wait a minute. Ginger, don't say anything to my Mom, okay? Not about anything. Not about Austin. Just say I fell asleep."

She smiled and patted me on the shoulder. "That's a deal, roomie."

As we started down the hill, I remarked, "You know, you've never been a good actor."

She didn't say anything, but held onto my arm. What irony, I thought. A year ago I was helping her through an emotional crises, and now here she was helping me down a hill, like I was an old lady. I pulled away from her.

"I can make it!" I snapped. "I don't need your help."

She stopped, looking me squarely in the eye. "I know you don't need my help," she said sharply. "But I wanted to try. I'm not playing games here. You're my friend and I believe you. Okay?"

I nodded. "Sorry."

She went on, "What do you expect? I come up there on the hill and you're on the ground, and I could tell you'd been crying. Did you think I would just walk away and leave you?"

I reached out and touched her arm. "I'm sorry, Ginger. You're too good a friend to get upset with me."

"Times two," she said.

"Times two," I repeated. Then, "Let's go down. It must be time for lunch or supper or something."

She grinned. "Sounds like the plan."

As we entered the kitchen, Mom was waiting, a look of concern on her face. "Abbie, are you all right?"

"She's fine," Ginger interjected. "Would you believe it? She fell asleep up there."

"Asleep!" Mom said, eying me suspiciously. "You just fell asleep?" Then she laughed, "What's with you, young lady?"

"Right now I'm hungry," I said, glancing at Ginger. "Both of us are hungry."

We sat at the kitchen table and made ham and cheese sandwiches. Then we heard Dad call from the living room, "What the Sam Hill's going on out there?"

Mom, who was holding the baby, stood up and hurried toward him. "What's wrong?"

"Why there must be a dozen cars out there in the field," he called.

Ginger and I exchanged startled glances.

"What's going on?" she said in a near whisper.

"Don't know," I said.

She got up from the table and went to the back window.

"Oh, Good Lord!" she cried. "Abbie, look at this!"

I jumped up, not knowing what to expect.

"Look!" she cried again, as she pointed toward the hill. "Those trees!"

Peering out the window I saw what she meant. The cherry trees were all in bloom, a blazing pink color! Despite the cold, they were in full bloom!

Ginger cried out, "No wonder the cars are stopping. They see it. That's a miracle, Abbie, if I ever saw one. That's a miracle."

Now Mom was back in the kitchen, shouting something about

the crowd and the trees and blooms. It swirled about in my head. The baby started crying. And the phone was ringing . . .

I walked by Mom in a daze, picked up the phone and said hello.

Someone from down the road was shouting about our trees. "Your trees on the hill are in bloom. Did you see? Did you see?"

"Yes. Yes. I know. I don't know why." Then I hung up.

I put the phone down and it rang again instantly.

Then Ginger was giving me a hug and laughing in delight. "See, this proves you saw him. It proves it. Tell your Mom. Tell everybody. Tell the world. You saw him. I told you I believed it. I told you."

She was more excited than me. I was still stunned from the afternoon. What was a little miracle compared to what I had seen? I sat at the table, chewing slowly on the sandwich, and staring at the back window. He had done that for me. He had done that for the others to see. And I smiled. I was at peace with the world.

Then Mom was back in the kitchen sitting beside me at the table. "Abbie," she said urgently, "do you know why those trees are doing that?"

"I think so, Mom, I think so."

She stared intently at me. "Why? Tell me."

"He was here this afternoon, Mom. I wasn't going to say anything, 'cause I know it's hard to believe. But he was. He did that to the trees." Then, I laughed. "No, he didn't, Mom. He had the angels do it. Just like you always said. Remember?"

She shook her head in bewilderment. Then she started crying.

I took her hand. "Mom, it's okay. You don't need to worry. It's okay. I saw him. He's not coming back anymore, he said."

Ginger came to the table, cradling Madeline Abigail in one arm. She put the other one around my mother's shoulders. "It's okay, Mom, your daughter is fine. Ain't nothing wrong with that girl, I tell you. She's A-okay."

Then Dad came back into the kitchen, a vexed expression making him appear a little older. "Abbie, what in the world is going on? Aaron Jefferson's out there and he says he saw you talking to an angel or something. What's he talking about? And there is a crowd out there in the field, and it's getting bigger."

Nobody said a word for a moment, then Mom said, "Jeff, did you look up on the hill? We may have cherries by tomorrow."

"What?" He went to the window and recoiled at the sight. Then he muttered, "We gotta do something about all those people. I'm calling the sheriff."

28

That night, December the twenty-third, a crowd of about two thousand persons gathered in the soybean field and serenaded us with "Silent Night" and "Away in a Manger" and other carols. The sheriff did send two cars out to control the traffic.

We sat in the living room drinking coffee and talking in hushed tones. Even Dad was certain that I had been in contact with someone divine. But we said little about it.

Ginger went to the window and peeked out from behind the drapes. She turned and reported, "They got some state troopers out there now. Good Lord, there's a lot of people."

We turned out the lights except for the ones on the Christmas tree. Several times reporters came to the door, but Dad said we didn't have anything to say. One asked if he could walk up the hill and take a picture of the trees.

Dad glanced at me and shrugged. Then he turned back to the man and growled, "Why not?"

Ginger chuckled and glanced over at me. "Sooner or later you're going to have to talk to the media people."

"I know," I said. "Maybe I'll refer them to Aaron Jefferson. He can tell them what he saw."

"What did you see this afternoon?" Dad asked. It was the first time he had spoken directly to me about it.

"Well, Dad, I didn't see a flying saucer," I said, smiling. Then, as serious as I could be, I said, "I saw Jesus, Dad. It was him. That's all. And he said that we should be helpful to one another, be friends in the spirit."

"Friends in the spirit?" Dad repeated. "And that's why the trees bloomed, I guess."

"I guess so. He wanted us to know he was here."

Mom said softly, "Well, we know it now. We know it now."

I smiled at her. "Mom, I guess I'll have to start going to church again."

She nodded. "I don't know, Abbie. Maybe that hill back there is like a church, after all."

Epilogue

On the day after Christmas 2005 the blossoms suddenly disappeared from the cherry trees. A small weekly newspaper had the only picture of them. They ran it with a caption saying experts could not explain why the trees bloomed, because the temperatures were far too cold for such an occurrence.

In the days that followed, there were news reporters and television crews coming into Winter Chapel. Most would stop at Pop Jackson's store and ask directions to our house.

Old Aaron Jefferson, the man who had been in the soybean field earlier that afternoon of December the twenty-third, was interviewed, saying he had seen me talking to someone who looked like Jesus Christ or an angel, and he had later seen the trees suddenly burst into bloom. He then told in great detail how he thought he was having a heart attack at the time.

Then the reporters would come to the house. After my holiday break was over, they would show up at UAB, trying to find me among the students. I would talk with them, telling them what I had seen, that I had an abiding faith in Jesus, and talked with him daily. Most listened with skeptical expressions.

In their reports they would emphasize that I "claimed" to have seen Jesus. Ginger called to say she was irked by these reports, but I didn't mind. As I told her, they were just doing their jobs and being objective.

On a sparkling March day in 2006, Ginger Burns and Glenn Lyons were married. They had the ceremony atop the hill at our house, because as Ginger told friends, "It is a sacred place." I was the maid of honor and wore a baby blue dress. Ginger was beautiful in a light yellow dress; a wreath of daffodils added a highlight to her burnished brown hair. Both of us wore sandals.

Ginger and I often bemoaned that we had not taken a picture of the trees during their blooming at Christmas. It just never occurred to us.

Mom and Dad still live in our old country house. They are as happy and crazy in love as any couple could be. Mom started a nonprofit group with Ginger's mother in a church near Winter Chapel. It is a small healing group devoted to families and friends who have been through hard times, whether it is a death in the family or teen pregnancy or anything else. Mom doesn't claim to be an expert, she just has a kind heart that wants to help people.

As for me, I finished my broadcasting communication degree and turns out, I did end up on TV, just not in the way I had daydreamed. It was no longer vital that I be the star anchor.

I now live in Atlanta. I know, it's a far jump from Winter Chapel, but I still make regular visits to see Mom and Dad. I now have my own talk show on PBS, called "Beyond." I live for my job, as I always wanted to do. It is a charitable foundation; we have famous people come on the set as guests (I got to meet Julia Roberts). We discuss everything such as world issues, Hollywood stars, our government, and even what the world will be like in the next twenty-five years. Our audience pays to hear and meet our guests and all profits are donated to the soldiers protecting this country and their families, and others in need.

As he said, we should "be friends in the spirit."

I suppose the reason why Jesus chose to visit me is somewhat of a mystery. Maybe we will all find out one day. Throughout this experience I have learned there are good and bad things that happen in life, but you just have to stay strong and never lose your faith; even when you don't think he is there, he is.

~